# MURDER
## *at the*
# CROSSROADS

////////////////////////////////////////////////////////////

*The dead cannot cry out for justice.*
*It is a duty of the living to do so for them.*

Lois McMaster Bujold

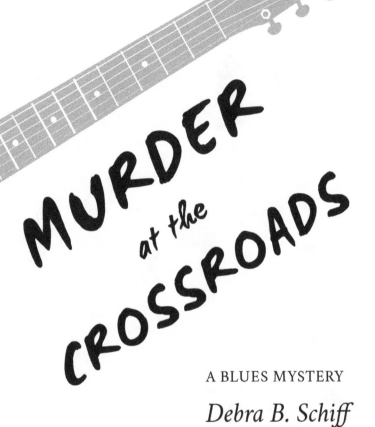

# MURDER at the CROSSROADS

A BLUES MYSTERY

*Debra B. Schiff*
*Doug MacLeod*

*To blues musicians and their fans—*
*past, present, and future.*
*And to all fighters for justice.*

# Acknowledgments

Debra would like to thank the following people: Miki Mulvehill, Doug's manager, for bringing my project to Doug's attention and helping to shepherd it to fruition; Doug Gordon, a patient editor, talented typesetter, and wonderful friend; Mikey Junior, a tasty harp player, for early encouragement; Doug Blaine, for his support and marketing savvy; Geoff Shannon, for the guitar icon; Cindy Rudy, an eagle-eyed proofreader and editor, who didn't let a pandemic stop her from helping a friend; and a special thanks to Stanley Platt, my beloved husband, for giving me time and space to write, even during a quarantine lockdown.

# CHAPTER 1

////////////////////////////////////////////////////////////////////////

**Eddie Baker** tentatively opened one eye and then quickly closed it to avoid the Los Angeles noonday sunlight streaming through the thin window shade. His throat felt like he had swallowed ground sandpaper, without a chaser. It had been an exceptionally late night at the small blues club where Eddie had been lucky enough to score a gig. It seemed everybody wanted to buy him a drink, and who was he to say no. He forced himself out of bed, despite a throbbing headache. The last song he had played last night, *Down Home Blues*, still reverberated in his head. Unable to face making breakfast and still wearing last night's whiskey-stained clothes, he stumbled down to the neighborhood convenience store. Some food and strong coffee would at least help him face the day.

"Good morning, Eddie," the store's owner, Mrs. Zhao, sung out. "The usual?" She was used to seeing Eddie a little worse for wear and didn't blink an eye at his disheveled state.

It seemed to be too much of an effort to open his mouth and form words. Eddie just smiled and nodded, which caused parts of his brain to painfully clank together.

"OK. Coming right up."

Hmph, musicians, she thought, as she gave the order to her husband to prepare. She would never let one anywhere near her daughters.

As Eddie stood at the store's counter waiting for his order, he idly looked down at a copy of the *Los Angeles Times*. He found himself staring at a picture of Earl Cooper, a face he hadn't seen since a night decades ago. A face he never consciously brought to mind but a face that had haunted his dreams for 30 years, since the night of July 12, 1962, back in his hometown of Ruleville, Mississippi. A night that had drastically changed his life and the lives of everyone he loved.

Back then, Eddie knew he shouldn't be traveling the back roads of Ruleville at night to his and Rosalynn's "spot," an abandoned shack down by the river. But how could he resist the plea she whispered in his ear after church that Sunday morning?

"Eddie, I just gotta see you tonight," Rosalynn had implored.

She wanted him—desperately—was all Eddie could think about. Rosalynn, the love of his 16-year-old life, who owed her luscious caramel skin and thick black curls to a Mexican grandmother. For her he was willing to face an ass whupping by his uncle and tongue-lashing by his aunt if he got caught sneaking back into their shared room in the middle of the night. But he'd face snakes, snarling dogs, hell, even the whole Klan that was supposedly everywhere at night, to see her. The thought of her warm body pressed against him drove his legs over the deep ruts in the rock-pocked road. It was all he could do not to break into a sprint. Luck was with him since there was a full moon to guide him. Even though he could hear some ominous rumblings in the distance, he figured he would make it to the shelter of the shack with time to spare.

Suddenly, the skies opened up. In the semi-darkness, with his mind on Rosalynn, Eddie hadn't realized the storm was right on top of him. It rained like it only could on a humid night in the

Delta, like the blues were raining down on him as Robert Johnson had so memorably sung.

He could make out the dim outline of some buildings on his right. It must be Ray Taylor's place. It was a not-so-secret fact that Ray was an active member of the Klan, so Taylor's farm was an area that Eddie normally gave a wide berth. Tonight, however, with the road turning to pure mud that was sucking down his every laborious step, Mr. Klansman's barn looked mighty good.

He cautiously swung the barn door open just enough to squeeze himself in. A horse nervously whinnied in his stall. "Whoa, boy," Eddie told the plow horse reassuringly. "I just want to keep you company for a couple of minutes." A lightning flash briefly illuminated the space. Besides a few bales of hay and a jumble of rusting farm equipment, there wasn't much to see. He was hoping for some old rags to dry himself off a bit.

Wait a minute. Was the thunder playing tricks with his hearing, or did he hear some men's voices outside the door? Could there be other fools out on a night like this?

"Move it," someone barked loudly. Shit, Eddie thought, that was definitely a white voice. He ran up the ladder to the hayloft as quickly as his shaky legs would carry him.

He flattened himself against the rough floorboards and peered through a knothole in the loft floor. The dark barn was suddenly illuminated by a couple of handheld lanterns that someone placed on a bale of hay. The light flickered across the faces of five white men. Eddie recognized Sheriff Cooper, Ray Taylor, and Everett Connors, the owner of Ruleville's general store and gas station, but not the two other men. The two strangers had to be brothers because they shared the same reddish hair and sharp features that reminded Eddie of foxes, foxes staring at a prey as helpless as a doomed hare. They were holding the arms of a man with a flour sack over his head. The hooded man had his arms tightly handcuffed behind his back, but Eddie glimpsed enough bruised tobacco-colored flesh to realize it was a colored man, a colored man in a whole heap of trouble.

He bolted upright. He had to be dreaming. Yeah, that was it, he had fallen asleep in the barn and was just having a bad dream. He rubbed his eyes and looked down again.

The scene below him was only too real. Everett had yanked off the sack to reveal the face of Lambert "Bertie" Johnson. At least it looked like someone named Bertie Johnson, except his right eye was swollen shut, distorting the rest of his features. Even in the dim light, Eddie could see Bertie's ashen color contrasting with the dull black and blue of fresh bruises. He could also see a thick rope ominously wrapped around one of Ray Taylor's meaty forearms.

Eddie was paralyzed. He could not even wipe away the water that was dripping off his hair and down his forehead. He was barely aware of it itching as it mingled with the beads of sweat on his chin to form a rivulet flowing down his chest. Wisps of hay were tickling his nose. He was breathing so hard he was sure that someone below would hear him, but everyone's eyes remained riveted on the sheriff.

"You wanted justice, boy," Sheriff Cooper said. "Well now, we're going to oblige you. It might not be the justice you had in mind, but it's justice just the same." The rest of the men laughed. Everett was grinning as broadly as if he had caught a thief red-handed grabbing candy in his store. Ray excitedly unwound and rewound the end of the rope.

"This jury," the sheriff continued while waving his hand to encompass the band of men, "which is definitely not a jury of your peers, because your nigga ass ain't ever gonna be a peer of ours, has found you guilty of disturbing the peace. We know ya came all the way down here from New York trying to rile up the local niggas up with all your talk of voting, equal rights, and all kinds of shit. You even had the *nerve* to put your hands on a white man. With the authority invested in me by the Almighty and the state of Mississippi, I proclaim the punishment to be death."

Ray eagerly tied a weight around the end of the rope and threw that end over one of the barn's rafters and reached up to grab it. Eddie could see the noose at the other end. Everett lined up two bales of hay directly under the swinging oval. The sheriff nodded at the two men holding Bertie. They lifted him on top of the hay and slipped Bertie's neck through the dangling noose. Bertie's legs buckled, but the two men held him up.

Eddie could feel the coarse rope burning into his neck as surely as Bertie felt it. If Eddie hadn't been lying down, he would have fainted.

A slight moan escaped Eddie's dry lips.

"You okay, Eddie?" Mrs. Zhao asked as she handed Eddie his fried egg and bacon sandwich and large coffee. "You don't look so good."

Eddie opened his eyes and realized where he was and that he had moaned out loud. "I'm fine, Mrs. Zhao, just had a rough night." But Eddie knew he wasn't fine and never would be.

**CHAPTER 2**

//////////////////////////////////////////////////////////////////////////////

**Mrs. Zhao** raised an eyebrow but didn't say anything when Eddie added the *LA Times* to his purchases. Eddie had never shown much interest in the news before. Maybe he'd finally been "discovered" and there was an article about him in it. She'd have to look through the newspaper later.

He balanced the breakfast sandwich and newspaper in one hand while trying to keep the coffee from sloshing over its lid in the other. As he confronted the barrier of a closed door and no free hands, another customer came in and provided him with an exit.

"See you soon, Mrs. Zhao," Eddie shouted on the way out.

Eddie returned to the tiny one-bedroom apartment he shared with his girlfriend, Sylvia Davis, on Wadsworth Avenue in South Central LA. It was actually Sylvia's apartment. Hooking up with Sylvia one night at a gig at Babe and Ricks Club had been a stroke of luck. He couldn't help staring at her velvety skin and beautiful smile as he played *Honest I Do*.

Eddie had gone to talk to her during the break. She was sharing a small table with a girlfriend. If she had a boyfriend, he wasn't around that night. And man, she was even prettier close up. For one of the first times in his life, he felt tongue-tied talking to a woman.

"Hi. I'm Eddie Baker. I'm with the band," was the best opening line he could come up with.

"Yeah, we noticed. I think it was the guitar that gave ya away," Sylvia coolly replied. Her girlfriend laughed so hard she almost spilled her drink.

"If ya give me your number, I'll come give you a private concert. Then you can hear what me and my guitar can really do, baby," Eddie replied, regaining his composure.

"Hmph," Sylvia sniffed. "I don't think so." She took out her compact and started powdering her nose, studiously ignoring Eddie.

Eddie returned to the stage crestfallen but determined. He managed to waylay Sylvia's girlfriend on her way to the ladies' room later that night and sweet-talk Sylvia's address out of her.

His next free night, he showed up on the sidewalk outside of Sylvia's apartment and serenaded her until she opened her window and stuck her head out laughing. He moved in with her a week later.

Eddie spread the newspaper on the scratch-marked kitchen table and perched on one of the wobbly chairs. Eddie absentmindedly sipped his coffee, his breakfast sandwich growing cold, as he read the article headlined "Justice Finally Arrives in Small Mississippi Town for 1962 Unsolved Murder." It seemed unreal, but there it was in black and white. An unnamed witness had finally come forward implicating Sheriff Earl Cooper in the Lambert "Bertie" Johnson brutal murder. The reporting hinted that other coconspirators might be prosecuted also. Maybe those white men would finally pay for their crimes, maybe they wouldn't. Eddie didn't have much faith in the Mississippi justice system.

He threw the newspaper in the trash. He took some small comfort blotting out Cooper's picture with a drizzle of leftover coffee before burying it under the greasy bag from his breakfast. The past needed to remain hidden. He had succeeded in hiding his past from Sylvia since they'd been together, and he didn't see any reason to share it with her now.

There had been many women in and out of Eddie's life since he left Rosalynn behind. In truth there had been too many one-night stands to count. But Sylvia was the total package: a fine-looking woman with a figure to die for, a steady waitressing job, and a convenient apartment. And she seemed to dig Eddie despite his middle-aged paunch and the strands of gray now starting to salt his close-cropped hair. Maybe it was the way he sang to her as he waltzed her around the apartment or the fact that he tried to make her happy. When he got home from work around 2:00 a.m., he would gently wake her when he slid into bed. Even when she pushed his hands away, which wasn't often, he still made her laugh telling her stories about whoever he played with that night.

The evenings they both had off, they might grab some mighty tasty barbeque at Mr. Jim's. His slogan was "You don't need no teeth to eat my beef." Eddie would do an imitation of a toothless grandfather gumming down some ribs that left Sylvia laughing so hard she gasped for breath. She also sensed when to leave him alone during his dark periods, when the demons of his past claimed him body and soul. Eddie would be paralyzed by guilt and self-hate, only able to sit in a chair with the lights off, downing glass after glass of cheap whiskey.

But mostly Sylvia and he had shared lots of good times together. Still, he knew the "honeymoon" period was coming to end. He had seen the signs, familiar to him from other relationships. Sylvia was getting tired of sharing the tips she made working the lunch shift slinging burgers at the Hamburger Hamlet. Some days she worked dinner too, especially when the rent was due. She'd come home after a double shift, kick off her shoes, collapse on the well-worn corduroy sofa, and start rubbing her feet.

"C'mon here, baby. Let me do that," Eddie would offer. He'd start at her feet and work his way up her beautiful curves, pausing to lick some stray ketchup off her neck. But even that was starting to lose its magic.

Now every day she had gotten to asking him when his music was going to pay some serious money. Since local gigs in LA were only paying $30 to $50 a night, he never was going to be able to flash the folding money needed to stay in her good graces. It was too bad, because after playing from 9:00 p.m. until the early morning, he could sleep in while Sylvia went to work.

While spending the rest of the day trying to block out the painful memories that Earl Cooper's picture had brought to the surface, he was relieved to find a gig that night playing with Clay Hammond. Clay was famous for being in the Mighty Clouds Of Joy gospel group, but now he was inspiring players like Eddie with more down-to-earth music. Eddie loved working with him because was a great songwriter and a great person to boot. He was only too eager to help Eddie after he heard the note of desperation in Eddie's voice when he called to ask if he knew of any gigs that night.

Not only did playing help take his mind off of things, but Clay Hammond's arrival at the gig gave him another story he couldn't wait to tell Sylvia.

"Sylvia, wake up. You ain't going to believe this one about Clay."

"Alright, Eddie. No need to shout," she said groggily.

"Me and the band were hanging out in front of the gig when we heard these noises that sound like gunshots about a block away. About 30 seconds later, here comes this beat-up old Ford Mustang coughing smoke, with three hubcaps missing. This beauty had two different colors of paint on the sides and its windshield wipers were goin' all kind of ways. It rattled into the parking spot. Clay turned off the ignition, but the car kept running and shaking for about 9 seconds before it finally died."

"You woke me up just to tell me about some kinda wreck of a car?"

"Oh, there's more. Then the back doors opened and three beautiful ladies with short, tight skirts eased out to the street. They got themselves together and 'sulter-ized' themselves into the club and sat down at the front row table."

"Them ladies better not have anything to do with you, Eddie," Sylvia interrupted.

"Of course not, honey. Hush now and let me finish."

"I said to him, 'Clay, let me ask you about that car.'"

"'You wanna buy it?' he said, looking a bit surprised."

"'No, I just got a question.'"

"'What's the question?'"

"Well, you know that car is kinda raggedy, shakes, and needs some work."

"Clay slowly nodded in agreement. 'Sure do.'"

"So how do you get those three gorgeous ladies to ride in that thing?"

"You know what Clay told me? 'The car got nothing to do with it.'"

Sylvia threw a pillow at him but couldn't help but laugh.

CHAPTER 3

////////////////////////////////////////////////////////////////////////////////

**The next day,** Eddie was back on the hamster wheel of struggling to find another paying gig. Maybe there was someone who wanted him to sit in at Shakey Jake's Safara Club or Smokey Wilson's Pioneer Club. There was lots of competition out there from other hungry musicians, but the old-timers seemed to like the way Eddie wielded his axe. He got christened "Sweet" Eddie Baker because he tastefully backed up the other musicians. And when his time came to solo, he was just what the song needed. Eddie took it as the ultimate compliment from other musicians that they told him he had a great sense of "taste and space." Some of that he had learned back in Mississippi and some he had picked up while playing in Chicago, his sanctuary for 10 years after he left Ruleville.

Eventually, he got tired of the Windy City's harsh climate and was ready to move on. When he got off the Greyhound bus from Chicago in 1972 and felt Southern California's brilliant sunshine on his face, he knew this would be his home. And once he was introduced to locals like George "Harmonica" Smith, Big Mama Thornton, Big Joe Turner, Pee Wee Crayton, and Lowell Fulson, Eddie felt like he had died and gone to heaven.

Twenty years later, many of those beloved icons had gone to the big jam band in the sky. The music scene might not be the same, but the warmth and sun were still there. The West Coast scene was cooking again with the influence of greats like Rod Piazza, James Harman, and the King Brothers. Touring bands like Charlie Musselwhite, Little Charlie and The Nightcats, and Sonny Rhodes brought their groove from Northern CA to SoCal. The new sounds emerging included everything from the acoustic blues of Robert Lucas, Doug MacLeod, and Bernie Pearl to the rock blues of Walter Trout and Coco Montoya. Janiva Magness' powerful voice was continuing the legacy of blues singers like Margie Evans and Mickey Champion. The promising future had energized Eddie, but now his own past was threatening to take his newfound joy away.

He was saved this day by a phone call from Lowell Fulson, asking if he could play with his band that night. Oklahoma-born, now California favorite son, Lowell Fulson had just released his *Hold On* album and was promoting it locally before going on a long tour. Eddie admired Lowell's strong singing, guitar playing, and songwriting. Eddie had been waiting a long time to score a gig with him. He liked playing Lowell's famous *Reconsider Baby*, a fervent plea to keep a lover, for an audience, but he'd hate to have to serenade Sylvia with it.

Backing up Lowell that night turned out to be one of Eddie's most powerful performing moments. Hearing Lowell on records was one thing, but when you played behind him, that's when you appreciated all the greatness that shone through every damn song. Lowell's music-making created a perfect storm of stirring lyrics, ear-grabbing melody, powerful chords, and soulful feel that swept over a grateful audience. Lowell had the crowd screaming, applauding, dancing, and begging for more. *That's what I'm talking about!* Eddie thought, after the set. It was like getting a graduate degree in blues music from one night at Dooto's in Compton.

But then it seemed to Eddie that playing the blues live always provided some kind of education about all kinds of folks. It was one thing to sing about taking another man's woman, but Eddie learned a valuable lesson about how dangerous it was to mess with what ain't yours while playing with Pee Wee Crayton. "School" was in session one warm, smoggy night in a rough club on Western Avenue near 54th Street.

The place was kind of small, with a long bar to the left of the bandstand. Tables with the accompanying chairs were placed about as if someone just threw them there. The dance floor was below and directly in front of the bandstand. There was so much smoke in the place that they kept the front door open for some fresh air, allowing the sounds of the cars and hustlers that lived on the street to drift in too.

Pee Wee called off a shuffle and the band commenced to rolling. Once the groove was locked, Eddie started looking out at the people in the club. One tall black woman wearing tight black stretch pants with a shiny little top really caught his eye. She was wearing silver high heels and her long hair was pulled up in a French twist tied with a silver comb. She had a way of walking to the ladies' room that made Eddie damn near forget the song. She was a thing of beauty to admire, but definitely nothing to mess with. At that time, he didn't realize just how prophetic that thought was.

Pee Wee was taking his time playing a slow blues, and the feeling was just getting better and better. Eddie noticed that "Silver Heels" started to dance with this guy in a nice-looking suit. Eddie couldn't keep his eyes off of her as she did a slow grind with the lucky fellow.

The crowd was going and everybody was having a good time. At the end of a fast shuffle, a guy walked up to Pee Wee and offered his hand. Pee Wee shook it, looked in his palm at a fat money bill, and then smiled and nodded to the man.

"Ladies and gentlemen, we got a request for a song I did a long time ago," Pee Wee announced. "It was for my hit record, *Blues After Hours.*"

A few knowledgeable blues fans applauded, but most of the folks had their attention elsewhere. Pee Wee hit the intro and the band fell into the groove of his classic slow blues. After a few choruses, "Suit" and Silver Heels got up to dance. Eddie loved the way she moved—not obvious and cheap-like, just subtle and with a whole lot of feeling. But all that feeling was soon to change.

A man in a work shirt, khaki pants, and work boots came in and started yelling some kind of "Ine" name like Pauline, Justine, or maybe Maxine. People kept moving out of the way as he made his way to the dance floor, like Moses parting the Red Sea. As he got closer, Eddie could see the man had anger and violence boiling in his eyes. Pee Wee was into the song, so Eddie hollered, "Hey P!"

Pee Wee looked at Eddie, real pissed off that he broke his groove, but then he realized Eddie was pulling his coat. He nodded and kept playing, all the while keeping one eye on the events taking place in the club. After a chorus, he nodded to the sax player to take a solo so he could keep both eyes on what was happening.

"Work Clothes" got to where Suit and Silver Heels were standing. They talked, and Eddie could tell that something was wrong. Suddenly, Work Clothes pulled out a knife and slashed at Suit. Suit ducked and turned his right shoulder to protect himself and got cut high on his right arm.

Pee Wee hollered, "Holy shit! We got a fight out there."

Silver Heels was screaming, trying to pull Work Clothes off of Suit. Some guys at the bar leaped to her aid. In seconds, all hell broke loose. A few people were laughing and acting entertained, while most of the folks moved away as the fight and cutting tumbled towards the bandstand. When the fight got too near them, the band stopped playing and guarded their instruments.

The bouncer finally got to the melee. He started to grab at folks, trying to pull the fight apart to get at Suit and Work Clothes. Silver Heels was free of the fight by that time. Her straightened hair had come undone, and a large slice of it stuck out like a fin on a shark. She sheepishly followed the rolling, fighting ball of men as it tumbled out the side door beside the bandstand onto the stoop that led to the side street. The fight stopped as the bouncer finally got Suit and Work Clothes apart. Silver Heels made her way out the side door to see what was going on. Pee Wee had put his Les Paul down and started to head to the door himself. Eddie figured he'd do the same, as did a few of the other guys.

When they got to the door, they saw the bouncer holding off Work Clothes while Suit was crumbled on the sidewalk. Silver Heels came through the crowd and when she saw the scene, she put her hand to her mouth and stared. Work Clothes broke free of the bouncer and took off down the side street.

Eddie felt an arm shoving him aside. It was the club owner. The owner asked the bouncer, "How is he?"

"Look like he cut, but it ain't bad," the bouncer replied matter-of-factly.

The club owner left and came right back with some bar towels and water and gave them to the bouncer.

The bouncer went to work trying to take care of the damage. It wasn't the first time he'd had to apply medical attention to some bonehead.

"Is he cut deep?" Pee Wee asked, peering over his shoulder.

"Nah, I don't think it's deep, but his suit sure is fucked up."

Pee Wee nodded silently in agreement. He turned to the club owner and asked, "You want us to take a break while you get this straight?"

"Hell no, Pee Wee!" the club owner replied. "This motherfucker ain't gonna die. We got a good crowd in there tonight. You and the band get to playin'!"

Pee Wee turned to Eddie and said, " C'mon."

Eddie followed him up to the bandstand. The drummer watched Pee Wee, looking for his cue.

"Hey everybody, get on your feet," Pee Wee sang. "We got a dance that can't be beat. We barefootin'."

The band rolled on with the tune and soon folks started dancing again. After a few more songs, things had returned to normal. Eddie looked for Silver Heels, but she was nowhere to be found.

That was one story Eddie didn't share with Sylvia. She might not appreciate him still enjoying the "scenery" from the stage. What she didn't know wouldn't hurt her, and his ass wouldn't get hurt either.

CHAPTER 4

Eddie was having the nightmare again where the hangman's noose was burning into his neck instead of Bertie's, except this time there was an angry swarm of bees loudly buzzing around his head. He awoke realizing that he wasn't hearing buzzing but rather an insistently ringing phone. He cracked open his eyes. The bedside alarm clock was showing 10:00 AM. Who in the good Lord's name would be calling him at 10:00 in the morning? All his bandmates and friends knew better than to call him before noon.

"Eddie, ain't you gonna get that?" Sylvia yelled from the bathroom where she was putting on her makeup.

He sleepily groped for the phone and croaked out a husky "Hello."

"Hi Eddie," rumbled a rich baritone with a honey-dripping Mississippi accent.

"Who's this?" Eddie demanded.

"What, you don't recognize your old friend Sonny?"

Eddie abruptly sat up in bed, bumping his head against the oak headboard. Sonny Jackson was a friend from Ruleville he hadn't spoken to in 30 years. When he abruptly left Ruleville, he didn't even have a chance to say good-bye to friends. The surprise phone call got his adrenaline flowing and he was instantly awake.

"Sonny, are you okay?" he asked, rubbing his head. "Are your momma and dad okay?"

"I'm fine, Eddie, just fine. Dad passed 10 years ago. Momma is doing okay. She's living with my sister Joyce in Houston. She's still making those sweet potato pies for church dinners that you said couldn't be beat."

Eddie could taste Miss Betty's sweet potato pie like he had just had it for breakfast.

"I'm sorry I haven't been in touch." He didn't know what else to say.

There was a pause on Sonny's end. "Well, that's all water under the bridge, water under the bridge. I'm calling to see if you're planning to come home to Ruleville for the trial."

Eddie's mouth was suddenly cotton dry. "What trial?" he managed to get out after swallowing hard.

"Why the trial of Sheriff Cooper. They finally got some good ole boy to testify. I thought you'd be interested."

There was silence on both ends of the phone.

"Ruleville is a different town from the one you left so long ago. Okay, it may not look all that different, but it sure does feel different. Did you know we had a black city councilman?"

"No, I didn't know that. I haven't really kept up with things."

"Well, I've kept up with you and your career. I know you're a popular sideman. You sounded great playing on Floyd Dixon's last album. That's how I got your number. I called some friends who called their friends, and well, here we are."

"I appreciate all the effort ya went through to speak to an old friend."

"And it was worth it just to hear your voice. But it's more than that." Sonny took a deep breath. "Look, truth be told, Eddie, I really called to ask you to come down for a visit. Maybe more than ask, maybe plead with ya."

"Sonny, I don't think that's . . ."

"Now hear me out," Sonny interrupted. "This trial's a big deal. It's already drawn national coverage. We're even thinking about chartering a bus to attend it. You may not be any kind of big-time star, but a lot of black folks around Ruleville are proud that a local boy made a bit of a name for himself. It would mean a lot to the whole community to have ya here. It would help prove that we're not afraid anymore. Maybe it would even help you. I know you were badly frightened by Bertie's death."

Eddie had never heard his light-hearted friend speak so passionately about anything. But Sonny didn't understand a fraction of what the fear really was. If only Sonny knew the overwhelming weight he'd carried around with him all these years, pulling his soul down, down, down. Drinking hadn't helped him escape the terrorizing memories, though Lord knows he'd tried to swim away from the fear through an ocean of whiskey. How that fear had dragged him so far down, that standing on the edge of a bridge in Chicago, looking into the depths of the tempting river, had seemed like a way up. Eddie had been too big a coward for that seemingly easy way out. Only playing the blues had provided a lifeline, had let him breathe enough to keep going, even with the noose always tight around his neck. How could he find the words to tell Sonny about his life without giving away his secrets, secrets that needed to stay buried all these years later?

Sonny had taken Eddie's long silence as indecision and kept right on talking.

"Plus, you're more than welcome to stay with me. I've been married 29 years. My three kids are grown and moved out, so I got plenty of room. I know my wife, Pearline, would love to meet you. I hope you haven't forgot your old bandmates. Luther is still in Mississippi but living in Jackson. Skeeter is working an oil rig in Broussard. What do ya say I get the old gang together? We could knock out some tunes and share some beers and laughs. That is, unless ya don't play with amateurs anymore. I guess we'd be a big letdown from the folks you usually play with."

Eddie felt trapped. He didn't want to come off as too high and mighty to play with friends, but even the thought of stepping foot in Ruleville, yet alone attending Earl Cooper's trial, had sent his heart racing. His palms were soaking wet. He needed time to think.

"Sonny, I need to check my schedule. Can I get back to ya?" He scrambled for a pen in his night table drawer and wrote down Sonny's number on the edge of an old utility bill envelope. "I'll call you back soon. Please send my love to Miss Betty."

He hung up the phone and let out a deep breath. It seemed the ghost of Bertie would not let him rest.

Since he had been jarred fully awake, there was not a chance he could go back to sleep. He pulled on the jeans that were on the floor next to the bed and slipped into a pair of flip-flops as he shuffled off to see if Sylvia had left for work yet. She was gone, not even waiting to see who had called. That was not a good sign. She hadn't turned on the Mr. Coffee for him either. Huh, it was going to be one of those days. He hummed Percy Mayfield's *My Mind Is Trying To Leave Me Too* as he started the coffee brewing before hitting the bathroom. As he washed his hands, he caught a glimpse of himself in the mirror. After talking to Sonny, he half expected to see the gangly teenager that had left Mississippi instead of the middle-aged man with graying hair and tired eyes that was reflected.

The memory of Miss Betty's perfectly spiced sweet potato pie lingered while he contemplated breakfast. The closest thing he could find to satisfy his craving was some cinnamon-flavored cereal. He poured the last of the milk in the refrigerator into a bowl of cereal and chased it with two cups of strong black coffee, liberally sweetened with extra sugar. With his belly full and his head clearing, he quickly showered and shaved. He managed to find a clean T-shirt to slip into. He ruefully noticed that the pile of dirty clothes in the corner of the bedroom looked ready to topple over. Uh-oh. Sylvia was definitely mad at him. Not doing his laundry was a clear signal of her displeasure with him. At least it beat the time she thought he had cheated on her and she had dumped all his clothes out the window. He would have to find time today to do some laundry and stop somewhere to pick up milk. She would be really steamed if he used all the milk without replacing it.

Eddie sat down at the kitchen table, pushed aside some unpaid bills, and contemplated his upcoming schedule. Luckily, or unluckily, depending on how you looked at it, he was not needed to play with anyone going on tour for another two months. He guessed he could juggle his local performances to leave room for a one-week trip to Mississippi. OK, I'm doing it, Eddie decided. He surprised himself with the decision, but once he made it, he was all in. He'd call Sonny later to let him know he was coming.

On top of scrounging for money for a bus ticket, he had to come up with some extra cash to pay for a present for Sylvia's upcoming birthday. It was bad enough being in the doghouse. If he didn't come through with a little something special, like that necklace she had been ogling in the window of Diamond Jewelry & Loan Pawn Shop up in Hollywood, he would find himself out on the street. He had slept in the street a couple of times and it made a doghouse seem like luxurious lodgings by comparison.

Who could he hit up for some work this week? Maybe Joe Houston, the great blues tenor sax player, had something going on. Eddie had sat in with Joe a couple of times before because Pee Wee Crayton had "pulled Joe's coat" to Eddie. Pee Wee's recommendation had been a big help. Eddie had even gone on tour with Joe once when his regular guitarist had cut his hand in a bar fight. He was going through a mental Rolodex of other possible musicians to beg for work when he heard some pebbles hitting the window.

"Yo, Eddie, are you there?" a voice boomed.

Oh shit. He had forgotten that he was supposed to go to Las Vegas today for some gambling with his friend Nick. Eddie opened the kitchen window and stuck his head out. Nick was leaning on his double-parked pickup truck. As soon as he caught a glimpse of Eddie he shouted, "Get dressed in your playing clothes and come down here, Eddie. We got a long trip ahead of us."

"I'll be down in a few," Eddie yelled. "I gotta pack."

Nick was the classic "jack of all trades, but master of none," although he could fix just about anything. He had enlisted in the Navy right out of high school, but he was too rebellious a soul to last there long. A confirmed hustler, he got by doing whatever made money—painter, carpenter, junkman, handyman, and some less honorable jobs. People were often put off by Nick's shaved scalp and heavily tattooed 6'4" of pure muscle, thinking he must be a skinhead. Nothing could be further from the truth. Eddie sometimes thought Nick must be a black soul reborn in a white body.

Eddie had first met Nick 10 years ago after they had both landed in the "drunk tank" after a night of heavy drinking, each sitting on opposite ends of the holding cell. Eddie was singing *Jailhouse Blues* with extra feeling. Nick tried to echo him. When a cellmate had told them to shove their singing up their ass, Nick drew himself up to his full height and calmly asked, "Is there a problem?"

The protestor, a tough-looking Mexican with a scar down his cheek, put his hands up and slowly backed up. "No, no problem."

Eddie looked over to see a white giant approaching him. Uh-oh, my skinny black ass is really in trouble now. He felt nausea rising in the back of his throat. Eddie looked wildly about for a way to escape. Everyone else—black, white, brown—had moved away. He closed his eyes and prayed. "Sweet Jesus, just don't let him break my hands."

Instead of the punch he had braced himself for, Eddie felt Nick enthusiastically pumping his hand. "Wow, man, I really like your singing. Can you teach me that song?"

Luckily for Eddie, blues fans are everywhere. The Nebraskan-born Nick Hayes was a blues aficionado who fancied himself the second coming of Howlin' Wolf, although Nick's mutt would be the one to howl every time Nick tried to sing. Once he learned that Eddie earned his bread from playing the blues, or at least *tried* to earn his bread from playing the blues, Nick sobered up and peppered him with questions.

"Who have you played with? What's your favorite Muddy Waters song?"

Before they were released, they had made plans to meet at a club that night. Eddie had found himself a guardian angel, or really a guardian devil might be more accurate. Nick turned out to be the perfect partner for the occasional jaunt to Las Vegas to play blackjack and pick up some change.

While it was not unusual for musicians to enjoy a craps game after a gig with the payoff burning a hole in their pocket, it was another thing to find someone who actually made money at it. Eddie had met James "Shakey Jake" Harris, the Arkansas-born harp player, in Chicago. When Shakey wasn't blowing harp with his nephew, Magic Sam, he supported himself gambling. His moniker came from the craps players' expression of "shake 'em."

Eddie had been watching a dice game in an alley behind a club one night, tempted to get into the action, when a voice behind him said, "Craps is a fool's bet. Blackjack is the only game you got a chance at."

Eddie turned around to see a smiling man leaning against a wall. When the man lit a cigarette, he recognized Harry Larson, the bartender at the club where he had just played.

"Oh, yeah? What makes blackjack better, Harry?"

"If you got any kind of memory and you can add numbers in your head, you can learn to play blackjack in way that actually gives you an edge over the house. It's based on mathematical probabilities. I do it in Vegas and make some nice pocket change." Harry pointed his cigarette at Eddie. "You gotta be careful not to be recognized by a pit boss or the 'eye in the sky' cameras monitored by security. The casinos don't truck with any card counting."

"Thanks for the tip, brother."

"Happy to help out someone who plays the blues as well as you do. You got a few minutes, Eddie? Come back inside and I'll show you what I'm talking about." The bartender stubbed out his cigarette.

Once back inside, Harry produced a well-worn deck of cards from under the bar.

"Lookie here. This is just an introduction to card counting. You keep a running count of cards as they are dealt by adding a point for cards 1–6, making 7–9 neutral, and subtracting a point for 10 and picture cards. A high count means the remaining cards in a deck are 10s and picture cards. You gotta memorize this chart that tells you what to do with the counts for each hand. Then you'll know whether to take a hit or stand pat and how to bet accordingly."

Harry quickly slapped a 10, 3, 4, 7, King, and 6 onto the bar. "So what's your count?"

"One," Eddie said tentatively.

"That's right. That don't mean shit, but you get the idea. Here's a copy of the chart to memorize. Buy yourself a deck of cards and practice, practice, practice. It ain't foolproof," Harry warned, "but if you follow the rules and don't get too greedy, you can actually come out ahead. I fly out to Vegas once a month. I'm saving up for my own club. Maybe you can play in it someday."

"Thanks, Harry. I hope your club happens soon."

"Good luck, Eddie."

Eddie might not have finished high school, but he was always good with math. It's funny, he thought, that so many musicians seem to have a knack for numbers. He turned to blackjack when he couldn't support himself with blues or pick up odd jobs with Nick. Nick would have accompanied him to Vegas just to ogle the showgirls and enjoy cheap drinks, but there were other perks. He would sit next to Eddie at a blackjack table and Eddie would help him play his hands, splitting the profits with him. Eddie didn't worry about carrying around a wad of cash when he had Nick at his side as a fierce-looking bodyguard.

When Eddie hit the street, Nick was busy working on a powdered donut. He held up a bulging bag.

"Want one?" he asked through a mouthful of pastry.

Eddie waved it off. Nick shrugged. He finished it off and then reached into the bag for another one. Eddie couldn't remember hanging out with Nick when he wasn't snacking on something. The big guy was the proverbial bottomless pit. The food buffets in Vegas lost money when Eddie treated Nick to dinner after a night at the tables.

"It's about time you got your lazy ass up. I've been up all morning working."

"You mean working on something besides those doughnuts?"

Nick pretended he hadn't heard that dig. "So, Eddie, you ready to make a little dough playing blackjack?"

"It's perfect timing. I'm desperate for some extra cash."

"Great," Nick replied, wiping his sugary hands off on his pants. "Let's go."

As they got into Nick's truck, Eddie caught a glimpse in the sideview mirror of the landlord walking to his building. Sylvia must have been a little short this month. Slumping down in the passenger seat, he whispered to Nick, "Get our asses out of here."

"Happy to oblige, brother." The old truck let out a squeal as Nick peeled out in a cloud of black exhaust. The landlord pivoted to trace the loud noise and started shaking his fist when he realized that he had just missed Eddie. Nick and Eddie were still chuckling 10 minutes later.

Eddie turned on the radio and settled in for the long drive through the desert. He could listen to his favorite station, KKJZ, until they reached the outskirts of LA. At least traffic was light on a Wednesday. If all went well, they'd be back on Friday with a pocketful of cash and plenty of time for him to look for a weekend gig. Card counting was hard work. He looked forward to getting back to playing music for some real fun.

Eddie and Nick had only played about an hour at a blackjack table at the Sands Casino when Eddie felt a tap on his shoulder. He waved it off, trying not to let it break his concentration. Then he felt a much sharper tap. When he swung around, a blank-faced security guard crooked a finger at him.

"Come with me."

"Hey, I'm playing here," Eddie said angrily. "I'm a good customer. Why are you harassing me?"

"Now!" the guard said, grabbing Eddie's shoulder. "You too," he said to Nick.

The guard squawked something into a walkie-talkie and led them to an elevator without another word. He escorted them to an office overlooking the casino floor and roughly pushed them into seats. The man sitting behind the desk didn't bother introducing himself. Eddie figured that the man's crisply tailored suit probably cost more than he made in a year playing music.

"We know you bozos have been cheating . . ."

"But card counting ain't cheating, sir."

"If I were you, I'd shut up and listen. This is a friendly warning. If we catch you at the Sands again, we're not going to be so friendly. We're going to let the other casinos know about you, too. If you value your health, you're going to stay out of Vegas."

"Now get them out of here," he said to the guard.

Eddie understood all too well the menace behind the "friendly" warning. He had some experience working for "connected" guys. One guy, who owned a club, really liked the way he played. Eddie believed he also liked him as a person. It turned out to be a good thing too.

One night he had gotten a call from George Harmonica Smith for a New Year's Eve gig in West LA. It was paying grand theft money, but Smith's regular drummer had signed on to another gig months before, so they had to find a replacement.

Eddie learned how hard it was to find a good drummer two months out for a New Year's Eve gig. Eddie asked everybody he knew and finally got the number of a jazz cat that had just heard his New Year's Eve gig wasn't going to happen. He said he could do their gig. Three weeks later, the other bandleader called the drummer and said the gig was back on. It was paying more than George's gig, so the jazz cat took it. Then he waited three days to call Eddie back. Eddie was screwed. By that time, there were absolutely no more decent drummers available. Eddie reluctantly called George to let him know.

"You better tell the man, Eddie. They some rough people."

Eddie mustered up his courage and went down to the club. He nervously asked the man if he could speak with him.

"Sure, Eddie. Come on into my office." He poured them both some grappa and asked, "What's on your mind, son?"

"Sorry, sir, but the drummer we got for the New Year's Eve gig just cancelled and we can't find nobody good enough to play with us instead."

The man frowned.

"But we could do the gig with a lesser drummer, or maybe a percussion player, or no drummer at all," Eddie hastily added.

The man didn't say anything. He just stared down at the empty glass of grappa.

Eddie started to panic. If one black guy didn't come out of that office or club, nobody would care. After a few minutes, which seemed like an hour, the man looked up.

"You have his phone number, right?"

"Yes, sir, I do."

"Give him a call," the club owner said very softly but deliberately. "Tell him if doesn't do New Year's Eve with George, it'll be next New Year's Eve before he'll even be able to pick up a drumstick."

So Eddie called the drummer and let him know who he was working for and what the man said. Not surprising, the drummer did the gig. And the motherfucker even showed up an hour and twenty minutes early!

Eddie had learned his lesson and was not about to cross one of those guys again, especially someone who didn't have a soft spot in his heart for him . . . or what passed for a heart in one of these cats. Even Nick realized that they were in a bad spot and meekly followed the guard out of the casino office without a word of protest.

"These gentlemen are checking out," the guard told the woman at reception. He followed them to their rooms, watched them pick up their still-packed bags, and then marched them out of the building.

"Now what?" Eddie said. "Sylvia's in a foul mood. I was counting on pressing a $50 bill in her hand when we got back. Plus I need money for the trip I told you about when we drove out here."

"We'll think of something, but can we at least have dinner before we drive back?" Nick pleaded.

A $1.99 steak dinner temporarily satisfied Nick, but it did nothing to brighten Eddie's mood. Whatever money he could earn playing music this weekend would just about cover his share of the rent and maybe let him put a down payment on a necklace. Getting money for a bus trip back to Mississippi seemed out of reach. It felt like *all* he ever did was hustle for money, Eddie thought wearily, starting with the day he first set foot in LA.

When he had arrived from Chicago in 1972, he was full of optimism that LA would be his big break. As arranged, Neckbone, a cousin of a friend, was waiting for him at the bus station. Neckbone had let him sleep on his sofa for a couple of nights while he showed him around town and introduced him to local players.

Eddie was amazed by the thriving blues scene in LA, but the blues scene wasn't all that impressed by yet another musician arriving from Chi-town. Eddie had to compete with lots of other talented blues players also hustling for work in Southern California. He did some odd jobs just to keep a roof over his head and some food in his belly while he took whatever gig came his way.

After working some rough-and-tumble joints, he gradually got good weekend gigs at the Parisian Room on La Brea with Big Joe Turner and Pee Wee Crayton. After word about his playing got around, Joe Houston and Lowell Fulson invited him along on weekend trips up to Oakland. Eddie scored some gigs out at the beach at The Lighthouse and Concerts By The Sea, which paid some long money. Cleanhead Vinson usually had something going on there. The bald-headed sax player earned his sobriquet after his hair was destroyed by a lye hair-straightening product. His clean head certainly didn't put off any women. His powerful voice along with his versatile sax playing proved irresistible. He bragged in *Cleanhead Blues* that he had what it took and didn't need hair. Eddie had learned some jazz and jump blues playing with him. Cleanhead's voice had been silenced forever in 1988.

William Clarke, the great harp player, was still alive and kickin'. Eddie could see if he could help him out. Oh, shit, Eddie remembered, he was out on tour.

If only Pee Wee Crayton was still alive. While he was a sweet man, he was far from an easy touch. He had to like you and know you from playing in his band before he could learn to trust you. To earn his trust, you had to be on time, never complain, and always, *but always*, act professional. Then if Pee Wee knew your story and he could help you, he would. But you couldn't mess with him. He always traveled with his security people: Mr. Smith and Mr. Wesson. Sadly, Pee Wee had passed away in 1985.

One of Eddie's best friends had been George "Harmonica" Smith. George had blown his harp with the likes of Muddy Waters and Big Mama Thornton. When George left this planet all too soon, Eddie not only lost one of his favorite people to play with, but a great teacher about life as well.

Damn. They didn't make harp players like that anymore. Well, maybe they did, and Eddie knew a successful one in Riverside, about an hour away from LA, who might be able to help him. It was worth a shot.

**CHAPTER 5**

Eddie hated just dropping in on someone, but he figured he had a better chance of getting money if he begged in person. The next day, he cajoled Nick into driving him on the 1-hour trip from LA up to Riverside. When Eddie flipped around the radio dial, he settled on George Thorogood and the Destroyers playing *One Bourbon, One Scotch, One Beer.*

"Oh, no you don't," Nick yelled. "Switch that off. They've destroyed a great John Lee Hooker song."

Uh-oh, thought Eddie, here comes another one of our seemingly never-ending arguments about what is blues music.

"John Lee himself took old blues songs and put a new spin on them," Eddie reminded Nick. "He'd have no problem with George Thorogood taking this song and putting his own stamp on it, as long as it boogied. And this song boogies."

"I don't care what you say. This is rock and roll, a different animal than the blues. It'll never be as good as *authentic* music. You know, like Delta and Chicago blues and jazz," Nick argued.

"Nick, I love you like a brother, but you can't lose what you never had. Yeah, I might dig the old-timers the most, but blues has to grow to expand its audience and to keep up with the times. Bluesy rock, bluesy jazz, bluesy funk, it's all good. I heard once that sharks have to keep moving to survive. Well, blues gotta keep moving forward too. That don't mean it forgets its past."

"When I wanna hear really good music, I wanna listen to unadulterated blues and true-to-its-roots jazz by the masters," Nick said stubbornly.

"Nick, back when Miles Davis did his *Bitches Brew* album, a whole mess of jazz people saw it as sacrilegious because of the electric piano and guitar. Not to mention the rock-style rhythms. Shit, now those same critics consider it a masterpiece."

"The blues is different. Stevie Ray Vaughn added all those notes, but he never improved on original Texas bluesmen like T-Bone Walker or Lightnin' Hopkins."

"You're a reverse racist, that's what you are, Nick. You don't think any white people can really play the blues. If the music comes from the soul, whether you're black, white, red, yellow, or polka-dotted like Buddy's guitar, it's blues music. You dig?"

They arrived at their destination, an unassuming red-tiled house, before Nick could reply.

"Please wait out here, Nick. No offense, but you can be a little, um, intimidating. I want my friends to give me a loan willingly, not under duress."

"And just who are you putting the touch on?" Nick asked. "You still never told me."

"You'll see in a minute."

When Eddie rang the doorbell, a lovely woman with a glorious cascade of silky blonde hair opened the door. It was Honey Piazza, wife of the great harpist Rod Piazza. She was a terrific musician in her own right; her electrifying piano-playing was an integral part of the Mighty Flyers band that backed up Rod's dynamic harp playing. Eddie and Honey had run across each other at blues shows and knew each other on a casual basis.

"Well hi there, Sweet Eddie. I guess you're looking for Rod."

"Yes, I am. Not that it isn't always a treat to see you, Miss Honey," Eddie hastened to add.

When Nick caught a glimpse of Honey, he leaned over and stuck his head out the window. Eddie was tempted to tell him to pick his jaw up off the driveway.

"Rod," she yelled over the Count Basie album playing in the background. "We've got company."

The elegant, thick-maned Rod appeared in the hallway.

"Well, this is a nice surprise."

Something about seeing Rod eye to eye threw Eddie off and kept him tongue-tied for a minute. Then Eddie realized it was the first time he had talked to Rod when he wasn't wearing the trademark sunglasses that he always wore on stage.

"I'm sorry to bust in on ya like this. Do you have a moment?"

"Sure. Why don't we go sit out on the patio and talk?" Rod responded.

"And bring that friend of yours waiting out in the truck," Honey added.

Eddie and Nick walked past a room filled with framed albums. Eddie had always been in awe of Rod's playing, starting with the days of his Bacon Fat band when he had a double harp sound with George Harmonica Smith. Now The Mighty Flyers had rocketed off with a heady blend of gritty blues, West Coast swing, jazz, and R&B.

They settled in on some patio furniture. Honey brought out a pitcher of iced tea. Eddie knew Rod had played with lots of mutual friends. Hell, you couldn't kick someone in the California blues scene without another musician rubbing his shin. Now was Eddie's chance to catch up on some of the cats he hadn't seen for a bit while working up to the reason for his visit.

"Nick, I don't know if you ever heard Smokey Wilson play his axe. He worked with Rod on an album for the Murray Brothers back in 1983."

"Yeah, Smokey's great."

"What's Smokey up to these days?" Eddie asked Rod.

"I hear he's been working on a new album, *Smoke n' Fire*. It's a good title for that fiery axeman. I hope it finally gives Smokey his due."

"Amen to that. Ya seen Johnny Dyer around?" Eddie knew the harp player because he had toured with his friend, George Harmonica Smith. Rod and Johnny had played together also.

"He's still blowin'. Best I know, he's hooked up with Rick Holmstrom for a new album too. That oughta be mighty tasty."

"Speaking of tasty players, Eddie, when are you going to record some solo material?" Honey asked.

Eddie grinned and shook his head. "Aw, that's not for me. I'm happy right where I am, lucky enough to be backing up some great talent."

"Well, never say never," Honey said with a smile.

"I don't want to take up any more of your time than I have to, so I'm gonna get right to it. I need to borrow $100 to go home to Mississippi for a bit. I don't know exactly when I can pay you back, but I promise I will, somehow or someway."

"Why of course, Eddie. Just give me a minute."

Rod came back into the room and handed him five $20 bills.

Eddie gave out a big sigh of relief.

"Now that you're here, do you want to sit in on a rehearsal?"

"Nothing I'd like better, Rod, but I'll have to take a raincheck. I need to get that bus ticket as soon as possible."

"I understand. Good luck."

"It was nice seeing you and meeting Nick," Honey said as she walked them to the door. "Maybe next time you'll be able to visit us at the new house we're building in Murrieta, horse stables and all. You're welcome anytime." She reached up on her tiptoes and gave Nick a peck on the cheek. For once, Nick was speechless.

CHAPTER 6

***Cash safely in hand,*** Eddie and Nick drove back to LA. This mighta been the easy part, Eddie thought. Now I gotta figure out how to break the news to Sylvia.

Nick interrupted his musings. "Too bad Honey seems so happily married. She's amazing. Did I tell you I was seeing a new woman, Marianne? She's a beautiful redhead who's also into motorcycles. I've taken her for a few rides on my bike. Lucky for me, she's not happily married."

Nick started describing their exploits in excruciating detail.

"Glad you enjoyed the trip to see Rod and Honey. That was a great Count Basie album they were playing," Eddie jumped in, trying to change the subject.

"Yeah, that was a hip album."

He and Nick had originally bonded over the blues. It looked like an appreciation of jazz was also going to be common ground. "You know, a lot of blues guys really dig jazz. Shit, Albert Collins was a big Jimmy McGriff fan," Eddie noted.

"The way I see it, it's a two-way street. Real jazz guys appreciate the blues. Duke Ellington, Kenny Burrell, Miles Davis, those cats were deep into the blues."

"Music is more than a two-way street. The most fun is when you travel without staying on any damn road."

"That's why it pisses me off that those asshole 'jazz almosties' don't appreciate the blues," Nick said heatedly.

"*Now* what bug's up your ass? What the hell's an 'almostie'?"

"Almosties ain't real jazz musicians; they're wannabe jazz musicians. These cats think blues is below them." Nick complained.

"Oh yeah, I've known a few of them. Did I ever tell you the story Doug MacLeod told me about a cat like that was filling in with him and George Harmonica Smith down at the Starboard Attitude in Redondo Beach? It's really stuck with me."

"Uh-uh, never heard this one. I'm all ears."

"You see this piano player was acting bored playing with George and them. His solos were all about showing off how much he knew, but he played with no feeling. On the breaks all he talked about was his 'big' jazz career. Doug told me after the first set, George leaned over to him and said 'Dubb, this is gonna be a long afternoon.' Well on the next set, an older couple asked George if he could play *I Left My Heart In San Francisco*. George turned to the band and said 'San Francisco in C.'"

"The piano player whispered to Doug, 'Does he mean *I Left My Heart In San Francisco?*'"

"'Yeah, that's what he means,' Doug answered."

"The guy says, 'Man, I gotta get my fakebook. I don't remember the bridge.'"

"So Doug tells him, 'You're a "jazz" guy, ain't ya? You got ears. You can fake it.'"

"The piano player panics. 'I don't think I can. Tell him to stall. I'll go down to the car and get the book.'"

"George immediately counted off 1, 2 and got the pickup notes to the top of the song."

"The piano player looked like he was ready to piss his pants.

Doug leaned over and told him, 'Don't worry man. Not only did George leave his heart in San Francisco, he left the bridge there too.'"

Nick laughed. "Good one! Now where was I? Oh yeah, so Marianne and I . . ."

Eddie tuned him out, turned up the volume of KKJZ, and let Nina Simone's version of *Just Like A Woman* wash over him.

"So, when you coming back?"

It took a few beats for Eddie to realize Nick had asked him a question and was waiting for a reply.

"Uh, I'm not sure."

"OK, brother, I'll see you on the flip side," Nick said when they pulled up back at Eddie's place. "And don't be too long. Sylvia might get lonesome and turn to a real man for some comfort."

Eddie laughed as he got out of the truck. "If Sylvia's taste in men is that bad now, you're welcome to her."

Sylvia jumped up as soon as he came through the door.

"Where ya been, Eddie? You've been acting kind of strange since you got that phone call the other day."

"I'm alright. Here's some money toward the rent," Eddie said, putting $40 on the kitchen table. "But we gotta talk, baby."

They sat down side-by-side on the couch. Eddie took Sylvia's hands in his and looked into her warm brown eyes. Her forehead was wrinkled in concern.

"That phone call was from my friend Sonny, back in Ruleville."

"Well, if he's asking for money, guess he's outta luck . . . unless you're holding out on me," Sylvia said, snatching her hands back.

"No, nothing like that. He wants me, not money. I can't tell ya about it now, but I promise to explain everything when I get back."

"Get back?"

"I just borrowed enough money from a friend to get a bus ticket to Mississippi."

"I thought you never wanted to set foot back in Mississippi. Whenever I've asked you about your past or talked about the South, you've just clammed up."

Sylvia was from a tiny town in Georgia. She didn't miss living in the South either, but she stayed in close touch with her mother and the rest of her clan of sisters, nieces, nephews, aunts, and uncles.

Eddie had been in touch with his aunt and uncle only a handful of times after leaving Ruleville. He didn't have a permanent address until he moved in with Sylvia, so it was hard for them to write each other. Those long-distance calls were just too damn expensive. At least that's what he told himself. It tore him apart to hear his aunt's worried voice in his ear. His uncle refused to get on the phone. Eddie couldn't figure out whether it was because Uncle Otis was bitter about Eddie leaving them in the lurch or if his uncle didn't want to reveal his true emotions about losing someone who had been like a son to him. Eddie sent them money once or twice, but he never seemed to have enough to spare. Eddie hadn't been there for them when they needed him most, just like he had let down Bertie and probably many others in his life.

He didn't realize how much he missed them until they were both gone, dying within a year of each other. He had only learned of their deaths when he ran into a musician from Ruleville whose parents had been friends with them. Eddie thought of them every time he played *Down in Mississippi*.

"I could be making a big mistake going there, but I have to finally figure something out." Eddie turned away. "It might help with some of my, um, dark moods."

Sylvia's expression softened. His dark moods just seemed part of the package of putting up with him, but sometimes they scared her.

He'd never told Sylvia about seeing the lynching. She'd told him that he sometimes talked in his sleep. He'd wake her up screaming,

"It's me you want, not him," grabbing at his neck. She'd hug him, feeling his cold sweat.

"Baby, you okay? What were ya yelling about?"

"Sorry. Musta been a bad dream about losing my mother."

"Uh-huh. Is there something wrong with your neck? You kept snatching at it."

"I must have a sore throat from smokin' too much. I gotta cut back. Let's go back to sleep."

If going back to Mississippi would allow him, and her, to enjoy more peaceful nights, she was all for it.

"I've talked to Nick. He'll be here if you need anything. Just don't get too friendly while I'm gone."

"I can take care of myself. Besides, if I get lonely, I'm sure I can do better than that overgrown puppy. When you leaving?"

"Tomorrow morning."

"Then I guess I better give you a little farewell party so you remember me while you're gone."

So this is really happening, Eddie thought to himself after the "party" was over. He turned on his side to do one of his favorite things next to playing music—watching Sylvia sleep. He wished he could be as peaceful as she looked.

## CHAPTER 7

A *menacing posse* of Klansmen is not waiting for me at the city limits was his silent mantra as he stood in line for the bus the next morning. After repeating it several times, he still wasn't convinced. It was hard enough to be a black man in LA in 1992. Trying to navigate life in the South posed daily dangers for all black people, not just him. Even with Sheriff Cooper in jail and Sonny's assurances, how safe was it really for him to go back? And then there was the not-so-small issue of facing Rosalynn. He purposely had not asked Sonny if she was still in Ruleville. They were supposed to get married as soon as she graduated high school. He hadn't exactly left her waiting at the altar, but they had an understanding. She had only agreed to their private "meetings" because of that understanding.

"I'm *not* turning out like my momma," she had told him the first time they stepped out. "Pregnant and alone at 15. Forced by her parents to marry my stepfather, a drunk who beat her. My life will be different."

He had broken his promise and never even told her why. Even as a teenager Rosalynn had a short temper and a long memory. The possibility of seeing her again scared him almost as much as seeing Sheriff Cooper in person.

His biggest fear, however, was that by returning to Mississippi, the Devil would finally collect on the debt that Eddie owed him—his life. Because Eddie knew, knew as sure as the sun would rise tomorrow in the east, that he should have been the one murdered that night, not Bertie. If he hadn't struck up a friendship with Bertie, Bertie would still be alive today.

Bertie had run into Eddie one night when the teenager was coming back from one of his rendezvouses with Rosalynn. Rosalynn liked it when he played his guitar just for her. Bertie stopped his car when he saw Eddie slowly walking along the road, toting his guitar.

"Hey. Want a lift?"

Eddie squinted at the driver.

"You're that Yankee, ain't ya? I heard you were here trying to stir up trouble."

"Guilty as charged," Bertie said with a smile. "But this is just an offer of a ride; no strings attached. I'm only a music lover who wants to help out a musician."

It was getting late and Eddie was tired. He looked up and down the road. The Yankee and he were alone. He climbed in.

"I'm Bertie Lambert."

"Eddie Baker."

"Nice to meet you, Eddie." Bertie looked over at the guitar sitting between Eddie's legs. "I don't suppose you're a Django fan?"

"Who?"

"Django Reinhardt. He's a great jazz guitarist."

"Nah. I'm a blues guitarist. You know, like Robert Johnson. You gotta be a fan of his."

"You got me there. I don't know that much about the blues."

"Man, you don't know what you're missing," Eddie said, shaking his head. "I never heard a colored boy talk like you. Where ya from?"

"I'm from New York City. You can blame my accent on that, and the diction on my English teacher. I'm on break from college, but I might never go back to school. There's too much work to be done."

"What kinda work?"

"Getting our people registered to vote. It's our right. And it's the only way things are *ever* going to change in the South."

"Maybe. But there's a whole lotta white people, white people with guns, who don't want things to change. I heard Loretta Hicks tried to register. Not only wasn't she allowed to register, but she was fired from her job. Then her house was set on fire and burned to a crisp. She had to move in with her son in Jackson."

"Nobody ever said it would be easy. But I'm not alone in this. The Student Nonviolent Coordinating Committee sent me down here to work with Fannie Lou Hamer. There's lots of good folks trying to change things—brave Negroes *and* brave white people."

Eddie sat there silently, trying to imagine what kind of white people would want to help colored folks.

"But enough about me. Tell me about your guitar playing."

"Pull over a minute and I'll show ya."

Eddie did an impromptu concert, including a song he had just learned, *I Believe I'll Dust My Broom.*

"That was fantastic! I never heard anything like that before. I wish I had time to really hear you play."

Eddie soaked up the praise. This Yankee was all right once you got to know him.

"Ya know, if you really want people 'round here to trust ya, the best way is to come to a party."

"I just might do that," Bertie said, rubbing his chin thoughtfully. "Where am I dropping you?"

Eddie hesitated. "I'd rather you didn't drop me off in front of my house. I know you mean well, but my uncle would have my hide for talking to you. Folks around here think you'll bring us more trouble than we have already. Just pull over here."

"I understand. No problem. Thanks for the concert, Eddie."

"Thanks for the ride."

Eddie started to walk away and then circled back to the car. Maybe he could do something to help without putting his neck out too far.

"Meet me here Saturday night and I'll take you to a little shindig I heard about."

"Sounds good. I'll see you soon."

Eddie did most of the talking on the drive back after the jam session Saturday night. He had been surreptitiously sipping moonshine between songs and was feeling nice and loose. Bertie was happy to let Eddie talk; he was hoarse from trying to talk to people over the loud music. He wasn't sure if he had made any converts, but at least nobody ran screaming away from him either. The car windows were rolled down so they could enjoy the fresh breeze after the house party's stale air. Eddie fiddled with the car radio dial, trying to find some blues music. He had just settled on a station when the music was suddenly eclipsed by a woman's frantic screams.

The screams were coming from a young colored woman pinned up against the side of a building by a mountain of a white man. Her blouse had been ripped off and was lying in the dust. One of his hands was holding a hunting knife to her throat; the other was battling to get up the struggling woman's skirt.

Bertie slammed on the brakes. He was sprinting out of the car before Eddie could stop him.

"If you make another sound, I'll cut your throat. Now just stand still you stupid bitch," the man bellowed at her. "It'll be over a lot quicker that way."

They each grabbed one of the man's arms and managed to pull him off of her. Eddie recognized the terrified face of Cora Mae Foster, a woman who sometimes hung out at the local juke joint. Eddie didn't know the white man, but guessed it might be Bear Connors,

Everett Connors' younger brother. Last time Eddie was in his general store, he had overheard Everett telling a white customer that his brother Bear had stopped by for a visit on his way home to Alabama.

"I haven't seen him for quite a piece. Is he still as ornery as a starving bear?" the customer asked.

"He's even bigger and meaner now, if that's possible. Maybe we should start calling him Grizzly Bear," Everett had laughed.

Huge. Ferocious. This man certainly filled that description.

The man was speechless for a few seconds, astonished that some colored boys had actually touched him. Then true to his nickname, Bear let out a bloodcurdling roar. He swung his massive head back and forth, unsure which of them to go after first.

Bertie turned his palms up. "Stay cool, mister."

Bear took a step forward toward Bertie, clenching the knife in his raised arm. His face was contorted with rage.

Eddie picked up a rock and got ready to throw it.

"No, no violence!" Bertie shouted to Eddie.

"We're not looking for a fight. Just let the woman go," Bertie said calmly to the man.

"What the fuck you say, boy!" Bear took another menacing step toward them.

Out of the corner of his eye, Eddie saw Cora Mae carefully edging away from them. She picked up her blouse and sprinted off into the woods, holding her blouse tightly against her chest.

Bear turned to look at the fleeing woman. While he was temporarily distracted, Bertie and Eddie made a break for the car. As they took off, Bear ran after them yelling. "You think you can run? You can't hide that car with them New York license plates. You're both dead niggas!"

Eddie and Bertie didn't talk on the short trip to Eddie's drop-off stop, each lost in their own thoughts. Eddie prayed that Bear couldn't tell him apart from any other local colored boy. Luckily,

Bertie never said his name. It had been dark, and it had happened so fast. Eddie was sure Cora Mae wasn't going to say anything. Whites wouldn't see a crime, and even the colored community wouldn't hold out much sympathy since she was walking alone at night. As if it was her fault that she had been attacked. It was Bertie and his car that Eddie worried about.

Eddie laid low the next couple of days, avoiding Bertie and any white people at all costs. News of an incident like this traveled fast in white circles. Eddie was sure that Bear had his own version of what happened that didn't include any assault against a colored woman, just two niggas trying to jump him. Eddie assumed Bertie, with his drive for voting rights, had been on the sheriff's radar anyway. But when the sheriff and his pals heard about the incident with Bear, it must have been the final nail in Bertie's coffin. That is, if they had dignified his death with a coffin.

Lord knows Bertie had been needed on this Earth to help their people. Eddie was just a dime-a-dozen guitarist. Why had Eddie been spared? He had asked himself that over and over again. Maybe he finally would get the answer by returning to Ruleville.

CHAPTER 8

**Eddie only** half-watched the scenery during the long bus ride from LA. His mind had drifted back to another trip he had made when he was also alone and frightened. That trip hadn't been made as he sat in a comfortable cushioned bus seat. He had watched the countryside unfold from Mississippi to Chicago as he peeked out of a boxcar, cold and hungry. He held onto his guitar for dear life to keep it from getting banged around. At every stop, he kept an eye out for any railroad bulls that would have loved to toss him off the train, and maybe worse. Miraculously, Eddie and his guitar made it to Chicago in one piece.

After Eddie got off the freight train in Chicago, he snuck around the tracks until he found himself in Union Station. The soaring limestone building was like nothing he had ever seen. It was filled with a mixed crowd of colored and white people in a hurry. That was something else he had never witnessed before. In Mississippi, if a white man walked down the sidewalk, the colored folks better get out of his way right quick. Eddie had seen an old colored woman knocked to the ground for not moving fast enough for a white man's liking.

The enormous station and swirling masses of people were enough to make him stop thinking about his growling stomach for a minute. But nature was calling in another voice. He walked around, looking in vain for the "Colored" bathroom. Eddie grabbed a porter rushing by.

"Excuse me, brother. Where's the Colored bathroom?"

The porter sighed. It pained him every time some arrival from the South asked him. "You in Chicago now, man. The bathrooms are for everybody. It's right over there," he said, pointing.

Eddie hesitantly went into the men's room, but sure enough, there were colored and white folks availing themselves of the facilities. Right outside the men's room exit, he took a deep drink from a water fountain. No "Whites Only" or "Colored" signs over it either. He wiped his mouth and looked around. Nobody was paying him any mind. But he didn't feel invisible like he did in Mississippi; he felt empowered.

Once he got out on the sidewalk, the crowds were even thicker than inside the station. He was almost deafened by the uproar of honking car horns and shouting pedestrians. Eddie swiveled his head from side to side, swept along by the crowds, until he swung his guitar case hard, right into someone's shoulder, knocking the blow's recipient right off his feet.

"Shit!" The curse came from a tall, solid-looking black man in a suit sprawled out on the ground. He refused Eddie's hand and sprang up quickly, dusting himself off and rubbing his elbow over his hat.

"Boy, you better watch where you're going with that thing!"

"Yes, sir. Sorry, sir," Eddie said apologetically.

The man looked Eddie up and down, taking in the dusty overalls and battered guitar case.

"Let me guess. Just fell off the cabbage truck?"

"Huh? Well, I did just get into Chicago a little while ago."

"Uh-huh. Got folks here?"

Eddie looked down at his scuffed shoes. "No, sir."

"So, what are you planning on doing here?"

"I figured I'd find the nearest juke joint and at least earn enough for something to eat and a room for tonight. After that, I'll have to look for some kind of job. If ya could point me in the direction of a juke joint, I would be much obliged."

"A juke joint. Let me guess, you're a bluesman."

"Yes, sir, I am," Eddie said defiantly. He didn't like the man's sarcastic tone.

"Okay, okay. No need to get yourself worked up. As a matter of fact, I'm a bluesman myself. The name's Willie Dixon," he said, thrusting out a scarred hand.

"Eddie Baker," he replied, gripping Willie's hand. A loud growl escaped Eddie's stomach.

They both laughed.

"Here's a few bucks, Eddie. Go to the lunch counter across the street and get yourself some food so we can all enjoy some quiet."

Eddie waved him off. "No sir, I can't take your money."

"It's okay. Tell you what, you can pay me back when you get your first gig. I'm going to draw you a quick map." He sketched out a rough street diagram showing Eddie the location of Maxwell Street. "Set yourself up there and you may make enough to get a flop for the night. You'll have a lot of competition there, though. I gotta hit the road. Here's the address for a friend, Muddy Waters, if you need help while I'm gone. Tell him I'm sending him another stray," Willie said with a chuckle.

Eddie didn't like being compared to any damn stray dog, but he knew he should be grateful for any help he could get. He blurted out, "Thanks a lot, Mr. Willie."

Willie just gave him a wave. After they parted, Willie turned back and yelled, "Hey country, let me hear you play sometime."

With Willie's map and the help of some patient Chicagoans, he was able to find his way over to Maxwell Street. He knew he must be close when he heard snatches of blues echoing down the streets. Maxwell Street, actually a giant open air market, had reached its peak in the '50s, but there were still plenty of musicians plying their craft there in the early '60s. The merchants lining the street liked having them there because they drew attention to their businesses. They even let musicians run wires from their stores to their electric guitars.

Eddie became accepted by other blues players who frequented Maxwell Street, including Robert Nighthawk and Johnny Young. He thought Johnny's mandolin playing was out of sight. The great Carey Bell was a fellow busker who occasionally blew his harp with Eddie. Eddie worked his way up from playing for tips on the street and at rent parties to finally working small clubs all over Chicago's South and West Sides.

Over the next 10 years that Eddie spent in Chicago, he'd often run into Willie Dixon. Willie was pleased to watch Eddie mature from an awkward teenager to a confident, accomplished musician. Eddie dug the blues scene in Chicago, but the bone-chilling winters took a toll on him. He often complained about the cold to a drummer from Texas named Tommy Lee. They had become friendly while crossing paths at various gigs. One particularly brutal night, they snuck into an alley to share a joint between sets. If they hadn't been drunk, they probably wouldn't have thought going outside on a night like that was such a good idea.

"I'm ready to leave this frozen hell of a town," said Eddie, barely holding the joint in his shivering hand.

"Man, I'm so tired of you saying that. Why don't you just leave already?"

"I don't know a soul outside of Chicago and Mississippi, and I'm sure not going back to Mississippi."

"Hey, you know, I got a cousin, Neckbone, who plays bass in LA," Tommy Lee said thoughtfully. "Every time he's in town he's always ragging on me, telling me how warm it is in LA. As a matter of fact, he's almost a homeboy of yours, born in Greenville, Mississippi. If you make it out to LA, I'm sure you can hook up with him."

Neckbone had been one more link in the chain of people who had helped pull Eddie through life. There was squabbling and jealousy like in any family, but the family of bluesmen looked after their own. Time and time again Eddie had been saved by the kindness of his fellow musicians. With no kin of his own to help, older bluesmen had taken pity on him. He had been passed along from Willie to Muddy to Neckbone to Pee Wee Crayton. And they had all added some spice to the gumbo of his playing.

He was coming back to Ruleville a changed musician, a changed man. Now he would find out if the people of Ruleville had changed too.

# CHAPTER 9

*Raelene Taylor* knew she'd get a whipping if she got caught hiding in the barn that July night, but she was willing to take that chance. The rumblings of the storm had woken her up. When she had looked out her bedroom window, she had seen a bunch of cars heading over to the barn. Something exciting was going on and dang if she was gonna miss it.

She had thrown on her clothes and noiselessly snuck out the back door. When she peeked into the barn, she saw her father, Sheriff Cooper, Everett Connors, and two strange white men. And it looked like they had caught a nigga like they was always talking about. With their attention focused on him, she had managed to slip into the barn and hide her 11-year-old body under some hay in the corner. It was one of the few times that she was glad she was small for her age. She wasn't scared when they strung him up; she was thrilled. She bit hard on her lip to keep from shouting with glee.

Younger by some 10 years than her married sister, the blonde, blue-eyed Raelene was her daddy's pet. When she went with him into town to run errands, people would greet them as "Big Ray" and "Li'l Ray." She liked it when there were meetings of the "Executive Committee" of the Klan at the farm. While her mother worked in the kitchen, Raelene would shyly serve beer and snacks to the men. Then she'd sit on the floor at her daddy's feet and listen to the men talk. She already knew that white people were the good, decent people and that the stupid, lazy colored people needed to be kept in their place. It was something she took for granted, like 1 + 1 = 2. One time during a meeting she had blurted out, "I hate niggas! I wish they was all dead!" The men had roared with delight.

"Looks like you're bringin' that one up right," the sheriff said approvingly.

Her father had beamed with pride. He still wouldn't take her to the nighttime meetings off the farm, though. If only she wasn't a girl.

After the men had left the barn, she had stayed hidden a good while just to make sure. Raelene was amazed to see some nigga teenager leave the loft and exit the barn. She got a quick look at his face, but she didn't recognize him. Not that she had ever talked to any nigga boys. Besides, they all looked alike to her anyway. The only thing she noticed about him was his soaring V-shaped eyebrows.

She was ready to race out after her daddy to tell him, but how could she explain why she had been in the barn? He'd really be angry that she had seen the lynching. Sometimes the men had stopped talking when she walked into the living room. When she asked her daddy about it, he had told her that womenfolk did an important job taking care of the men; they were too delicate to know the rough things men did to protect them.

Raelene kept her counsel and watched her daddy more closely than usual the next couple of days. Life went on as normal. She put that nigga teenager out of her mind. He had a helluva lot more to lose by coming forward than she did. She was sure if he even tried to say anything, the Klan would find a way to keep his mouth permanently shut.

CHAPTER 10

As **Eddie** got off the bus in Ruleville, he raised his left hand to shield his eyes from the sun, trying to get his bearings. There was a scattering of cars waiting there to meet the disembarking passengers. He was uncertain which one to head to until he heard a familiar voice shouting, "Eddie, over here!"

The voice belonged to a heavyset, cola-colored man leaning against a faded blue Caprice with plastic taped over the driver's-side back window. He sported denim cutoffs and a Saints T-shirt stretched over a generous belly.

Eddie picked up his travel bag and guitar case and quickly walked over to the man, feeling the late afternoon Mississippi sun beating down on his neck. He had forgotten how hot his native state was. He squinted at his childhood friend, trying to find the teenager within the balding, middle-aged man waving at him.

Sonny wrapped his friend in a warm bear hug. "It's great to see you." He stepped back and gave Eddie a once-over. "Ya look pretty good . . . for an old guy."

"You look good too. I see that wife of yours hasn't been starving ya," he said, playfully poking at Sonny's stomach.

Sonny nodded. "Pearline's a mighty fine cook. I'll give her that. Of course I keep her filled up with the good stuff too," Sonny said grinning broadly, while wagging his pelvis in a circle.

They both laughed.

"C'mon." He grabbed Eddie's things and somehow found a place for them in a trunk already stuffed with a variety of rusted auto parts. "We got a lot to catch up on." He gave the passenger door a big slam after Eddie slid into the taped vinyl seat. "That door can be a little tricky."

Sonny kept up a running commentary on the way to his house, driving with one hand and pointing to buildings or waving at people with the other. He paused in front of a two-bay garage with several cars parked on the oil-stained driveway.

"That's my auto repair shop. I know it don't look like much, but it pays the bills. I lost all the white customers when I first bought it from old Mr. Connors, but they started coming back about 10 years ago. You remember the Smith twins?" Sonny didn't wait for an answer. "Well they moved to Detroit and worked for GM for over 25 years. I heard they retired to Florida. I told you that Luther moved to Jackson. Last I heard, he's managing some kind of boutique. Skeeter is in Louisiana working on the oil rigs. He's back to visit family every chance he gets. As a matter of fact, he's in town now and said he would like to get together with us. I know you remember Gloria, or at least her glorious tits." Sonny smiled and licked his lips. "She's a widow and the music director at the church. It does make sitting through Sunday services a little more bearable. There's no missing church since I married Pearline. Rosalynn is still in town," Sonny said without missing a beat, slipping a sideways glance at Eddie. "She never married, but she had a son, EJ, hmm, less than a year after you left. Rosalynn works most days at Sullivan's Supermarket, if you're interested in seeing her." Eddie was saved from commenting by their arrival at Sonny's house.

It was an old but neat two-story house with royal blue aluminum siding and a porch with an old-fashioned chair swing and pots of red geraniums along the stairs. Sonny's shop had featured a graveyard of old cars and scattered parts. Obviously, the house was Pearline's domain.

When Sonny opened the front door, Eddie was overwhelmed with smells he hadn't enjoyed for over 30 years: home-cooked cornbread and collard greens.

A pumpkin-shaped woman with a broad forehead framed by short curls came bustling into the small foyer. Her huge smile radiated so much warmth that it melted any fears Eddie had about imposing on Sonny and his wife.

"Well, Eddie Baker, I'm so happy to finally meet ya. Sonny has told me so much about you. And knowing Sonny, about half of it's probably true."

Eddie laughed and reached out his hand. Pearline grabbed him instead and gave him a bear hug almost as strong as her husband's.

Pearline turned to Sonny. "Now why are ya standing there grinning like a hound dog who just found a long-lost bone? Take the man's bags up to Nathan's old bedroom and let him settle in before dinner. We'll be ready to eat in about an hour."

"Yes, ma'am," Sonny with a mock bow.

"C'mon, Eddie. If ya survived some hobo dinners on the way to Chicago, you can probably survive one of Pearline's meals." He quickly ran up the stairs before his wife could get in another word.

An hour later, Eddie was called down to a table groaning with Pearline's delicious down-home dinner of Southern comfort food. Eddie's mouth drooled while they held hands and said grace.

"Wow, I must be some special kind of guest, or do you and that no-account husband of yours eat this well every night?"

"I used to cook for a houseful of people. With the kids scattered, I don't get to feed people like I like to. It's nice when the whole family gets together over the holidays," she said wistfully.

"Your kids don't live nearby?"

"Nathan, that's the oldest, he's a dentist," Sonny said proudly. "Him and his wife and their two boys live in Atlanta. Teddy, the middle child, he's got his own insurance business up in New York City. He's married with a little girl."

"That's my baby, Ruth," Pearline said, pointing to a photograph on the sideboard of a pretty young woman in a college robe. She's working on her master's degree in nursing in Baltimore. I miss them all terribly, but we made sure our kids got an education so they could get out of Mississippi."

"Sounds like they did all right."

"Yes, with all praise to Jesus."

"Jesus and a lot of damn hard work," Sonny muttered under his breath. "Now you know what we've been up to." Sonny eagerly leaned into the table toward Eddie. "I've been waiting a good long time to talk to you. What else have ya been doing, besides playing music?"

"Look, Sonny, ya know ever since I was a kid, all I wanted was to play music. Shit, it ain't easy, but for me if I had to be in some kinda office 8 hours a day, work construction, or some damn factory line, that shit would've killed me."

"You be careful with your language now, baby," Pauline chided him.

"I'm sorry, Pearline."

"That's alright, baby. Here, have some more fried chicken. You ain't gonna go hungry in here."

"Yeah, but it's been worth it, right?" Sonny asked, taking a drumstick for himself.

"I don't know, man. When I'm working and got the rent made and food on the table, it feels right. But when things get light . . ." Eddie shook his head.

"Mmm-hmm. I got what ya mean, man."

"And when I see what you and Pearline got," Eddie said, waving his left arm to encompass the sideboard covered with framed family photographs and the platefuls of food on the table, "well, it makes me think."

"Yeah, but when you on the stage making great music, that's got to be some kinda natural high you can't get anywhere else," Sonny insisted.

"Nothing else like it for sure, Sonny. When I know my music is reaching people, maybe making them feel a little better about their lives, that gives me some kinda purpose. It's like, I'm where I should be and doing what I'm supposed to be doing."

"But it's got to be something else, brother, when everybody is looking at you up there. I'd like to know what that's like. Nobody pays me no mind around here," Sonny said, flashing a grin at Pearline.

"Oh, hush. Nobody pays ya no mind only when you actin' the fool," Pearline said fondly.

"Yeah, that's what you might think, man, but let me tell you something that Luther Allison said: 'Leave your ego, play the music, and love the people.' See right there, man, that takes you out of it. It ain't about you, it's about the music and the people."

"Man! Luther was speaking some serious truth there! And that's the truff with 2 ff's."

"Who's Luther Allison? He some kinda preacher?" Pearline asked as she passed Eddie a pitcher of lemonade.

Both men laughed so hard that the pitcher shook, almost spilling some of its contents on the table.

"Sorry, Pearline. I didn't mean to laugh at ya. Luther's a great bluesman. And I guess all bluesmen are preachers 'cause they damn sure preach the truth."

"Speaking of some serious truth, what do ya think's gonna happen with Sheriff Cooper's trial?" Sonny asked, suddenly switching gears.

"Your guess is as good as mine," Eddie said. An image of a gloating Sheriff Cooper floated above Sonny's right shoulder. Eddie closed his eyes and wearily rubbed his temples.

Sonny seemed to think Eddie had an inside track on the legal proceedings. Even Pearline's sharp elbow to her husband, which Eddie pretended not to notice, didn't seem to faze him.

"The truth is finally going to come out about what happened back in 1962. Ain't that right?"

"Sonny, don't you see the man is tired," Pearline finally exploded. "You two will have plenty of time to talk some other time."

"It's okay, Pearline. Honestly, I didn't know nothin' about the trial until I saw an article about it in the LA paper. But I'm curious, how are they going to convict Sheriff Cooper after all this time?"

"They got someone named Rusty Miller to testify."

"I assume Rusty got his name because he's a redhead," Eddie said casually, as he helped himself to another piece of cornbread.

Sonny and Pearline exchanged a look that Eddie couldn't read. "What makes you ask?"

"His name just sounds familiar," Eddie mumbled through a mouthful of cornbread.

"Assume so, but I never saw a picture of him. But it seems him and his brother Wade actually were there when Bertie got killed. I heard those two were a sorry pair of peckerwood meth users, but Rusty finally got himself right and wants to testify to make up for his life. You know, part of that 12 Steps bullshit. Mark my words," Sonny said, pointing the stripped drumstick at his friend, "if that's all they got, the sheriff is gonna get off. There are still plenty of Klansmen around who can serve on a jury. They got a fancy new name, the White Citizens Council, but they still the Klan. Just 'cause they're not dressing up in sheets on weekends don't mean they think Bertie's death was a crime. It's a damn shame they got Bertie's family's hopes up after all this time."

Eddie pushed away his plate. He suddenly wasn't hungry anymore.

"Pearline, that was a fantastic dinner. I'm stuffed."

"I know ya have room for a slice of my pecan pie."

"Maybe next time. If ya'll excuse me, I think I'll grab a smoke outside."

"Sure, Eddie. Go on out to the back porch. I'll come keep you company in a little bit," Sonny said.

Eddie went upstairs and grabbed his guitar. He opened the screen door onto the back porch and made himself comfortable on one of the porch steps. There was a full moon, just like the night he left. And now that he was back after all that time, nothing seemed to have really changed. He thought he had changed, that he was ready to battle the Devil face to face and win. Because if Sheriff Cooper wasn't the actual Devil incarnate on Earth, he was surely Eddie's demon. Fight the Devil? Hell, he wasn't even ready to fight whiskey and start playing sober, although a doctor had warned him that he was slowly but surely killing himself with alcohol. At that moment, he wanted a drink more than he ever had.

As if the Devil had read his mind, Sonny appeared carrying a brown bag.

"Thought you could use a drink," Sonny whispered. "Just don't let Pearline know. She don't hold with no liquor in her house. I got this corn liquor from a bootlegger in return for a brake job. I usually keep it hid in the garage, but I smuggled it home to share."

"Sonny, you're a friend indeed." Eddie took a gulp from the bottle and started choking. "Shit! I forgot what this stuff is like."

"How can you forget something as soothing as mother's milk?" Sonny asked with a grin as he took a generous gulp from the bottle. He looked down at the guitar in Eddie's hands. "Why don't ya play me something?"

Eddie started playing his favorite Robert Johnson song, *Cross-*

*roads.* An unremarkable guitar player from a small Southern town, the young Robert Johnson had disappeared for a while. When he returned, he played like nobody's business and went on to be crowned king of the Delta blues. Legend had it that his guitar mastery was a gift right from the Devil, whom he had met at midnight out at the crossroads. Of course, he had traded his immortal soul for that gift. Eddie wasn't sure about the Devil part, but Johnson's burning vocals sure sounded like he had been to Hell and back.

Sonny took his harmonica out of his pocket and joined in as Eddie sang. One of the lyrics asked the Lord to have mercy and save his poor soul.

But would the Lord have mercy on his soul? Eddie wondered as he played, or was he already damned for all eternity for not helping save poor Bertie?

CHAPTER 11

Eddie shuffled downstairs yawning. It was early, mighty early by West Coast and bluesman's time, but he didn't want Sonny and Pearline to have to tippy-toe around him in the morning. Pearline was carrying two bowls with the remnants of soggy cereal over to the sink when Eddie entered the kitchen.

"Good morning, y'all," Eddie said, stifling another yawn.

Sonny, wearing a denim work shirt with his name stitched over the pocket, was heading toward the back door.

"Well, look who's finally up," he said with a broad smile.

"Did ya sleep okay, sugar?" Pearline asked, handing Eddie a mug of coffee.

"Like a baby. I forgot how quiet it was here."

Sonny gave Pearline a quick peck and paused in the doorway.

"So Eddie, got any plans for today?"

Eddie knew he was a coward when he left Ruleville all those years ago and he knew he was a coward yet. As a teenager, incredibly full of himself, he had assumed that Rosalynn urgently wanted to see him the night of Bertie's death because she craved him as much as he craved her. But over the years, he wondered if something else was going on. Could she have needed to tell him something important, like she was pregnant? If so, why had she never let him know? After he walked out on her, Rosalynn could have turned to his Auntie Alma for help. Alma and Rosalynn's mother were old friends. Rosalynn was almost a surrogate daughter to her. He had never told his aunt about his and Rosalynn's relationship because he didn't think his aunt would have approved. As much as she loved Eddie, she had subtly, and sometimes not so subtly, let him know she never thought he would amount to much. She wanted a better provider than a musician for "her" Rosalynn. But knowing his aunt, she would have made sure to get word to him about a baby. She didn't truck with men who didn't stand up for their responsibilities.

Eddie still wasn't sure he wanted to hear the truth, but it was now or never to speak to Rosalynn. He remembered Sonny had told him that she worked part time in the downtown Sullivan's Supermarket. That seemed like neutral ground to face her.

"I need to take care of some, um, errands downtown."

Sonny pulled a ring with two keys out of his pocket. "Here," Sonny said, tossing Eddie the keys. "There's an old Plymouth sitting in the garage. Feel free to use it while you're here. It ain't much to look at, but it still runs. Sort of like you, brother."

"Thanks," he said, ignoring Sonny's dig.

"Need anything from the grocery store, Pearline?" Eddie asked.

"Naw, I'm good. But that's sweet of you to ask." Pearline looked inquiringly at her husband, but he just shook his head.

"Good luck," Sonny said. "Call me at the station if you need anything."

Eddie tried to keep calm by listening to the radio during the short drive. Music, any kind of music, helped him get his mind off of things. He drove around to the store's rear, parking near the employees' entrance. There were a couple of workers milling about, enjoying a cigarette break. Rosalynn was there, the silver strands in her hair only making her more beautiful. His heart missed a beat. All that time thinking about her, all the million and one things he wanted to tell her had filled his head for 30 years. Now that she was here in the flesh, he didn't have a clue what to say. She glanced over when she heard the car door slam. If she was surprised to see him when he approached her, her expression didn't give her away.

"Hello, Eddie," she said as she calmly ground out her cigarette stub in the sand-filled bucket by the door. It was as if she had been expecting him to meet her at work that day.

"Hello, Rosalynn," he managed to say.

"I heard you were back in Ruleville."

"Damn. I forgot how fast news travels in this town. Is there somewhere we can talk?"

"Sorry, I have to get back to work, and I don't think we have much to talk about."

"After all these years you're still *that* pissed off at me? I'm sorry I left without a word to you. Really I am. I woulda thought that by now you would have forgiven me and moved on with your life. Maybe if you had married someone else . . ."

"What? You think I'm still pining over your sorry ass? Humph." She spat on the ground, just missing Eddie's shoe. "I do have a life, and you're certainly not part of it in any way, shape, or form."

"What about EJ?"

"You know my son's name? What about him?" The question hung in the air as she turned her back on him and entered the store without looking back.

Man, you are so stupid. You couldn't have messed that up any more than you did, he chided himself. After he got into the car, he slammed the door so hard the old Plymouth shuddered. Shit, shit, shit! He banged the steering wheel until his hands stung.

Now what? Think, Eddie, think. And show some balls for a change.

He walked around to the front of the supermarket and went in, spotting her on Register 2. Luckily, there was only one person in her line. He grabbed a Coke out of the drinks cooler and got behind her customer. After the customer left, Rosalynn rang up Eddie's purchase without a second look.

"That'll be $1.50 for the Coke, sir."

Eddie slowly counted out $1.50 in quarters but hesitated before handing it over. "We are going to talk about EJ. I have a right to know if I have a son."

Rosalynn's eyes flashed. "You have no damn rights. If you think you can sashay in here and take away my son, you got another think coming."

The store manager, distributing some rolls of change at the next register, looked over when he heard Rosalynn raise her voice.

"I don't think you want to make a scene here," Eddie said, nodding in the direction of the manager. "Meet me at 7:30 tonight. You know where. If you're not there, I'll be back." He grabbed his Coke and receipt and was past the register before she had a chance to say anything else.

Just talking to Rosalynn for a few minutes had been a painful experience. The sweet, loving girl he had reminisced about seeing was gone. Eddie sat in the car, sipping the Coke and longing for some rum to go with it. He raised the bottle in a mock toast, "Here's to buried memories." As soon as the words left his mouth, he remembered another toast, another burial of sorts.

Once Ray Taylor had taken down Bertie's limp body, he and one of the red-headed brothers had roughly carried it outside, giving it no more respect than they would a sack of potatoes.

"This deserves a drink," Cooper crowed, brandishing a hip flask. He raised his arm in a toast. "To my favorite kind of nigga, the dead kind."

"To dead niggas," echoed Connors, taking a deep gulp from the proffered flask.

Sheriff Cooper and Everett Connors left with their arms around each other's shoulder, sloppily pounding each other's back. Eddie heard doors slamming and then cars driving off. He strained his ears, but the only sounds he heard were cricket chirps and the horse rustling in the hay. He waited a few minutes to make sure the coast was truly clear. A wave of dizziness washed over him when he sat up, his heart beating wildly. Eddie fought back the urge to vomit. As stunned as he felt, he knew he better haul ass in case anyone came back to the barn. Those men would be just as happy to have *two* dead niggas to dispose of. Through sheer willpower, he got his numb legs to climb down the loft ladder in the dark as quickly as he could. There was no way he could still go on to meet Rosalynn. It would only endanger her if he had told her what he saw.

The storm had ended as quickly as it had started. Eddie cautiously poked his head out of the open barn door. No one was in sight. A few straggler clouds scuttled by, leaving the moonlight to shine brightly through the clear skies. The sweet, rain-washed air hit his nostrils but couldn't hide the stench of his sweat-drenched clothes.

He left the barn and started to walk back home, hugging the pine and dogwood trees lining the edge of the road. Every time he saw a headlight or thought he heard a car, he pressed even deeper into the landscape, sometimes walking through tangles of under-brush. By the time he got home, his face and hands were badly scratched.

He used his usual late-night entranceway into the house, noise-lessly slipping in through a back window into his portion of the bedroom. His aunt and uncle on the other side of the room did not stir.

Eddie's parents had divorced when he was barely a year old. He never saw his father again and didn't remember anything about him. The only remnant of his father was a man in a faded black-and-white photo who shared Eddie's narrow, V-shaped eyebrows.

All his mother, Ruby Jean, had told him was that his father felt it would be easier to be poor by himself than be poor and try to feed two more mouths. His mother had died 7 years later from rheumatic fever. Eddie's mother's sister, Auntie Alma, and her husband, Uncle Otis, had taken him in. They were childless, having lost their only daughter to the same rheumatic fever that had claimed Ruby Jean's life.

Some of Eddie's fondest memories of his mother were hearing her sing in the Mt. Zion Baptist Church choir. His Auntie Alma added her lovely soprano there every Sunday. Eddie assumed he got his flair for music from them. He grew up against a backdrop of gospel songs always playing on the radio, the only kind of music Alma would allow in her house. When Alma wasn't around, his uncle would hastily spin the dial to find stations playing blues, R&B, anything he could pick up. It didn't matter what kind of music they caught snatches of—country and western, Delta blues, Cajun, Texas two-step—Eddie soaked it all up. His exposure to the blues would form deep roots, but the seeds of other types of music were also planted and stayed buried right beneath the surface.

Eddie's earliest attempts to make music were strumming away on a diddley bow. A diddley bow is just a string stretched between two nails on a board. After a while, he was ready for a better sound. He had seen a lot of guitar players playing with a slide. Eddie found a piece of copper pipe, got his uncle's pipe cutter, and made himself a slide. He would never be confused with Son House, but he now could at least play with some feelin'.

One day, his Uncle Otis thrust a used guitar at him.

"Here. If you're going to make all that racket, it might as well sound more like music than damn caterwauling," he had said gruffly.

Eddie knew that his uncle had scraped together money for the guitar from the little he made as a sharecropper. It made the gift even more precious. Slowly, slowly, chord by chord, he taught himself to play the guitar by ear. He was careful to play only gospel songs around his aunt. He liked it when she sang along. Whenever his aunt wasn't around, he'd practice the songs he heard being played by old-timers on porches, drifting out of juke joints, or briefly heard on forbidden radio stations. Eddie begged for lessons from friends' fathers or grandfathers. None of them wanted to be bothered. They were only too happy when Eddie finally found a real teacher and left them the hell alone.

Eddie heard about him one night when a couple of musicians Eddie knew by sight but never talked to were coming out of a juke joint. One of them was a drummer. He was so short you could barely see him over his drum kit. The other guy was a bass player, tall and skinny as a poplar sapling. If you looked at them together, you could not help but think of Mutt and Jeff. Eddie shamelessly trailed behind them eavesdropping, hoping he could learn some inside dope from a couple of real musicians.

"You know that old man back in the woods, plays guitar," "Mutt" said. "I can't 'call his name now. But you know who I mean."

"Jeff" nodded. "You mean that old man with the loose eye, Otha."

"Yeah, that's him. That cat can play!"

"Sure as hell can. It's been a long time since he's been 'round, though."

"Um-hum. It's a shame. Well, I gotta book. Talk to ya later."

Mutt and Jeff split at a fork in the path they had been walking. Eddie took a chance and chased after Jeff.

"Yeah, what you want, boy?"

"I play a little guitar. How can I meet that man you were talking about?" Eddie asked timidly.

"Shit. You wanna meet Otha?"

"Yeah, I wanna learn how to play," Eddie said more forcefully.

"Well, I don't know if he want to teach nobody, much less see nobody. He just lives by his-self in a small house back in the woods.

So deep in the woods, today arrives tomorrow." The bass player chuckled to himself.

"Is that why he never plays around here?"

"I heard he gave up playing blues because his wife died. He wants to be with her, so he just playing gospel now. Why you wanna bother him?"

"Mister, I'd do just about anything to learn how to play better. The only way to do that is learn from the best." Eddie stared at him with pleading eyes.

"Alright, alright. If it's so damn important to you, here's what you do. Go down the old state road. Right after the gas station, there's a road to the right. Take that road 'til you come to this big magnolia tree. Turn right again and it'll take you to him. But don't say I didn't warn you."

The next day, Eddie rushed home from school, grabbed his guitar, mumbled an excuse to his aunt, and went to see Otha. There was only one house where the directions led. It sure enough was way back in the woods. Eddie nervously knocked on the front door, but there was no answer.

"Mr. Otha, you home?" Eddie yelled.

The only response was some squawks from a crow roosting on the pine tree shading the house. Maybe that bass player was right, maybe Otha don't want to be found, Eddie realized as he reluctantly retraced his steps out of the woods. But I want to find him. I *need* to find him.

Eddie tried again the next day. This time, when he approached the house, an old man was sitting in the weather-beaten rocking chair on the porch. He looked none too happy to see Eddie.

"What you doing here, boy?"

Eddie held out his guitar. "Mr. Otha, I want to learn how to play. I hear you're the best around here."

Otha nodded. "Maybe you heard right. But I ain't no damn teacher. Ya gotta feel the blues, and I can't learn ya that."

Maybe that wasn't the whole truth. Looking into Eddie's eyes, Otha saw himself when he was a young pup in Jackson and approached Delta bluesman Ishmon Bracey for help all those years ago. Ishmon hadn't turned him away. For Ishmon's sake, he should give the boy a chance.

"Well, I got nothin' to do anyway. C'mon in. Let's see what ya got."

"I only know a little bit so far." Eddie played Leadbelly's *Good Morning Blues*, one of the songs he had laboriously taught himself. It wasn't perfect, but he played it with as much feeling as a 16-year-old could muster.

"That ain't half bad. Let me think on it a bit. I'll let ya know."

Eddie later learned that "ain't half bad" was high praise indeed from Otha. But that day, he went home feeling pretty dejected. He tossed his guitar into the corner and didn't have the heart to touch it for a couple of days.

Otha went about his business the rest of the day, not giving Eddie much thought. That night when he crawled into his lonely bed, Otha offered up a prayer.

"Lord, this is Otha. You know all I want is to go to heaven and be with Lucy Anne. I been playing just the gospel since she gone. But there's this boy and he's good, and one day he can be real good. He needs to know what I can teach him. And I'm thinking that might be the right thing to do. If you don't agree with this, would you let me know? Give me a sign or something. Amen."

The week went by and Otha was still waiting for his sign. Otha prayed again for guidance.

"Lord, I'm still waiting."

After a bit, Otha still didn't get a sign, not even an owl's hoot. So Otha continued, "Well, since I ain't heard from you that it would be wrong, I'm guessing it's alright." Otha turned on his side to go to sleep and then he added, "But if it ain't alright, let me know. OK?" He closed his eyes and went to sleep.

Otha never did get that sign. The next time he went into town to get supplies, he left a message at the church for Eddie to get in touch with him.

At least twice a week Eddie rushed through his chores and ran off to see Otha. Otha taught him enough new gospel songs to appease Auntie Alma. Uncle Otis was impressed by how much Eddie's playing improved and let Eddie be. Eddie found himself letting Otha learn things about him that he never shared with anyone, not even Rosalynn. Some of it he told Otha; other things he just let his guitar speak for him. Otha never exactly told Eddie he was glad that the teenager had shown up, but he was eagerly pacing the porch on the days Eddie promised to come and seemed reluctant to end each lesson.

Eddie started feeling so confident after six months of lessons that he let himself daydream of being a sought-after blues musician, maybe even being asked to make a record one day.

"Mr. Otha, you ever make a record?" Eddie asked after his next lesson.

"Why you ask that, boy?"

"I don't know, just wonderin'."

Otha sat back in his chair and looked thoughtful. After a long pause, he replied, "You from here originally, ain't you, boy? So you know what it was like when you coming up."

Eddie nodded. He had a feeling Otha was gonna tell him something important, so he leaned in to catch every word.

"Well, my time was worse, son. Seem like every day you see strange fruit. I remember one day I was with this gal, long before I met my wife. It was back in my rascalin' days, if you know what I mean," Otha said with a wink. "I met her at this juke I was playing and we hit it off. End of the night, we went back to her place and took a 'nap,'" Otha said with a mischievous grin.

Otha paused to see if Eddie got what he was talking about. Eddie got it alright and smiled back at him.

"Well, we was laying up in the bed in her little house late the next morning, just easing into the day, when there was a knock on the door. She got up to answer it, peeked through the little crack in the door, and saw a white man in a suit with an automobile outside. She came back to the bedroom and told me there was a white man at the door that come in a car. I got scared, boy."

"I said to her, 'Don't go back to the door yet, give me a bit to get gone before you see what he want.'"

"I put on my clothes, climbed out the back window, and started walking in a straight line to the woods. I made the woods alright, hid myself, and waited just about an hour, I believe. Then I eased back to the house. The automobile was gone, so I figured the man was gone too. He was. I went back into the house to get my guitar. I was so scared, I'd left it there."

"'What that white man want?' I asked the gal."

"He want to find you to make a record."

"That was my chance, boy. Ain't never had another one since."

Eddie was determined that if someone came to ask him to do a record someday, he'd make sure he talked to the man. He told his Uncle Otis that if a strange white man ever came lookin' for him, to ask if it was about making a record.

His uncle had roared. "I don't think you gotta worry about that for a long time yet. And if a strange white man comes to the door, none of us are gonna stick around to talk to him. That's for damn sure."

One of Otha's most valuable lessons was that blues is a lot more than three chords. One time in LA some asshole who heckled the band throughout their set came up to Eddie during a break.

"It's only three chords. Shit, anybody can play that," the man said sneeringly.

"No, they can't," Eddie replied emphatically. "And that's why I'm up on stage playing and you ain't. Hell, you even had to put down some cold cash for the privilege of hearing me play those three chords." Eddie looked over his shoulder. "I don't see anybody wait-ing in line to pay to see you."

"Yeah, you got that right," another band member hooted.

Mr. Heckler just sputtered and walked away. Score one for Mr. Otha.

After seeing Bertie's murder, Eddie's first reaction was to run and tell Otha what he had seen. He stopped himself in mid-stride. There was no sense in upsetting an old man. There was nothing Otha could do. Otha was already weighed down by all the lynch-ings and violence against colored people he knew about over his long lifetime. His uncle and aunt had more than their share of trou-bles in life, just by virtue of living in rural Mississippi. After all their kindness to him, Eddie was determined not to add to those troubles. He had no one to turn to. He'd never felt so alone since right after his momma died.

Eddie crawled into bed, totally exhausted, but it was useless to try to sleep. Every time he closed his eyes, he saw Bertie's swinging body, his neck twisted to one side, a puddle of urine darkening the pale straw. Bertie's eyes had been staring out at nothing, but Eddie was sure they were searching for him, pleading for help.

It wasn't like he didn't know about lynchings. A classmate's cousin in Georgia had been strung up in the '50s because he'd sup-posedly sassed a white woman. The body had been left there for days, with flies buzzing around it, until his family could secretly cut him down and bury him. But it was one thing to hear these sto-ries and another thing to see the sickening violence right before his eyes, especially against someone he knew.

The morning after Bertie's death, Eddie feigned illness and stayed in bed all day. If Auntie Alma noticed his scratched face, she kept it to herself. It was Uncle Otis who roughly shook him awake the following day to tell him about Bertie's body being found. Eddie acted shocked when his uncle broke the news to him.

"Did ya know that boy?" he asked Eddie.

"We were kinda friends. He gave me a ride once, and I took him to a house party. He wanted to hear me play, but he also was trying to get people to register to vote."

His uncle looked at him suspiciously. "Why you wanna mess with someone like that?"

"I felt sorry for him. He seemed kinda lonely. Besides, I never met a colored boy who talked like him."

"Yeah, and look where it got him."

Bertie's body had been wrapped up and weighted down with rocks and then thrown into the Sunflower River. Somehow, the corpse had floated back up and was discovered by a fisherman.

The coroner noted it as "Accidental death by drowning." Bertie was hastily buried in an unmarked grave under the excuse that his family didn't want to bear the expense of having his body sent back to New York. Bertie's family tried to find out what had really happened to him, but local law enforcement built a solid wall of denial they couldn't breach. All the colored folks in Ruleville knew the truth but were powerless to do anything about it.

"I think I'll go out back to practice a bit. It'll help me clear my head," Eddie told Uncle Otis that morning the body was found.

"You do that, boy."

Once outside, Eddie listened at a knothole as Uncle Otis and Auntie Alma discussed the murder in low tones. Otis must have told her that Eddie knew the dead boy because Alma suddenly raised her voice in alarm.

"I'm scared, Otis. They may not stop at some Yankee boy. What if they come for our Eddie next?"

"It'll be alright. We'll keep Eddie under wraps for a while. We'll get through this," Otis said reassuringly.

When Eddie went back inside, Auntie Alma was bustling around the kitchen as if nothing had happened, but she avoided looking directly at him. Uncle Otis put on the "mask" he wore around white folks and smiled at him.

"Eddie, I'd appreciate it if you didn't go see Otha today. I, um, need you to help me with some chores."

"OK, Uncle Otis."

That night, Eddie made his move. He waited until he heard the rhythmic breathing that let him know his aunt and uncle were asleep. Fumbling in the dark because he did not dare put on a light, he found the old, rope-handled bag he had used when he moved in with them. He hastily packed his meager wardrobe: three pairs of underwear and some socks, an extra work shirt, and his church shirt and pants. He knew he had exactly $5.60 in small change he had earned in tips from playing. He grabbed his guitar and threw it over his shoulder. He held his breath while his uncle changed positions, but relaxed when he heard Otis resume his steady snoring.

He groped for a piece of paper and a pencil and took it outside to write so he could use the moonlight.

*I'm mighty sorry to leave like this, but I got a ride up North and gotta take it tonight. You know I had talked about leaving Mississippi someday. I gotta leave now. It ain't safe for any colored boys here. I will write when I'm settled. Love, Eddie.*

He propped the note in front of the coffee canister where he was sure his aunt would see it in the morning. He grabbed a couple of biscuits and wrapped them in his handkerchief for the road. Eddie looked around the small house that had been his home for 9 years and tried to memorize every detail, from the newspapers stuffed in the cracks to the faded red and white checkered tablecloth. He knew he might never see the house, or his aunt and uncle, again.

Since a ride was just a figment of his imagination, he would have to jump on a slow-moving freight train. Passenger service on the Illinois Central RR that served the Ruleville Depot had ended in the 1950s. He didn't have money for a nonexistent ticket anyway.

There was really no place to go but Chicago. He wanted out of the South. He didn't know a soul in the Windy City or know much about the city itself, but he knew that at least it was friendly to blues musicians. A steady migration of Delta bluesmen had left the South and contributed to the Chicago sound. Maybe there was room for Eddie Baker to contribute to it too.

## CHAPTER 12

//////////////////////////////////////////////////////////////////////////////////////

**After seeing Rosalynn** at the supermarket, Eddie drove past Sonny's shop and kept going. He wasn't in the mood to talk to anyone. He was relieved when he entered Sonny's house to see a note addressed to him on the kitchen table from Pearline.

> *I'm at a prayer meeting and then we're going to visit some sick church members. Help yourself to the leftover chicken and whatever else you want in the fridge.*

Eddie nibbled on some chicken without really tasting it. He wished he had a bottle of Pabst Blue Ribbon—hell, a six-pack of beer really—to wash it down with, but he was too short on funds to make a run to the liquor store. Eddie grabbed his guitar and went into his room to practice for a couple of hours. He played one of his favorite songs, *Broke Down Engine Blues* by Blind Willie McTell. By the time he heard Pearline return, he felt relaxed enough to go down and talk to her. He could smell coffee brewing as he entered the kitchen.

"It's wonderful being of service to the Lord, but I'm about done in. I was just sitting down to a cup of coffee. I made some extra. Wanna join me?"

"Sounds good."

"Ya get your errands run?"

"Mm-hm," he replied, pretending to be engrossed in adding milk and sugar to his coffee.

Pearline got the hint that Eddie didn't want to talk about his day. She tried a hopefully safer topic. "So what was Sonny like when ya'll were growing up?"

Eddie searched his memory for a story he could share, one that wouldn't get Sonny into *too* much trouble.

"Did Sonny ever tell you about the time he put a frog in his sister's bed? She almost jumped out the window."

"Lord no, but that sure enough sounds like him."

"He probably didn't want to tell you the best part. Joyce got hers by putting a snake in one of his boots. He put his foot in the boot and screamed so loud that his poppa came running in with a shotgun in his hand, thinking they were being attacked by the Klan. And Sonny was the one who got his ass whupped from here to Sunday, not Joyce."

"That explains why a country boy like him is so 'fraid of snakes. Nathan brought one home to show him, and Sonny went running out of the room like his hair was on fire."

They were laughing so hard they didn't notice Sonny as he entered the kitchen.

"Glad you're having such a good time with my woman."

"You don't mind if I kidnap her and take her back to LA with me, do ya?"

"Suit yourself, but I don't see you as a regular church-goer."

"Well, I might find religion yet. For now, Pearline's cooking makes me think I've died and gone to heaven already."

That night Eddie tried to keep focused on another one of

Pearline's fine dinners and Sonny's jokes, but all he could really think about was meeting with Rosalynn.

"So, you got your clean sheets for the Klan meeting tonight?" Sonny asked.

"Yeah, sure," Eddie answered, as he pushed some black-eyed peas around his plate.

Sonny's roar made Eddie jerk his head up. Pearline was punching Sonny in the shoulder, who was laughing so hard that tears were running down his face.

"I'm sorry, what did you ask?"

"Boy, you sure ain't with us tonight. I bet this has something to do with a woman. Is it one back home, or is it somebody we know?"

Eddie's face felt red hot. "I really need to talk to Rosalynn, though I'm not sure she's willing to talk to me. I asked her to meet me at 7:30."

"Well, that sure enough explains it. Good luck."

"Pearline, your dinner was delicious. I promise next time to clean my plate. Let me make up for it by helping ya with the dishes."

"Now don't you go setting a bad example, Eddie," Sonny said.

"Humph," said Pearline as she snapped a dish towel at Sonny, who managed to duck just in time.

"You go ahead now, baby. I'll save you some ice cream for when you get back. You might need some sweetness before the night is out."

"Thanks. You are way too good for that good-for-nothing husband of yours." He gave Pearline a kiss on the cheek on the way out the door. She laughed and shooed him out the door with her dish towel.

Sonny had casually mentioned that Sheriff Cooper's nephew, Matt Cooper, was now sheriff. "He ain't like his uncle," Sonny had assured him. But then again Eddie had read that it was the Sunflower County DA's office with the help of the Feds, and not the current sheriff, who had built the case against the old sheriff and his accomplices. The new sheriff was content to let sleeping dogs lie.

"If you stay out of trouble, it ain't likely you will even meet him while you're in town," Sonny told him.

Since arriving back in Mississippi, Eddie had kept telling himself "You are safe. You are safe." That mantra emboldened him enough to take a drive out to the Taylor farm. He thought that if he could survive that, maybe he really was safe.

As Eddie approached the Taylor place on the way to his meeting with Rosalynn, he felt compelled to stop, even though every fiber of his soul resisted it. The empty fields testified that it was no longer a working farm. A car was parked in the driveway and the grass around the house was neatly cut, so somebody was still living there. The barn, or at least a skeleton of a barn, still stood. Everything about the site of Bertie's murder had changed, yet nothing had changed. Any paint on the barn had long been weathered off the splintered wood. The parts visible from the road were covered with kudzu, which filled in the gaps of the missing planks. Grass and weeds grew unabated around the building's boundaries and up to the road, attesting to the building's abandonment. Seeing the barn in its current decrepit state did not take away the scene's pain; it still had an incredible power over him. Bertie's death enveloped it like a ghostly shroud. Eddie knew that the barn would still be with him long after the last piece of rotten wood had disintegrated in the Mississippi sun. The words "Feel like a lucky man to get away with my life" from *Down in Mississippi* by J.B. Lenoir echoed in his mind as he started to drive away.

With his thoughts on the past, not the present, he hadn't noticed the sheriff's car coming up the road, kicking up clouds of dust along the gravel road. The car's siren woke him out of his reveries, and he immediately pulled over.

The man in a crisp sheriff's uniform who walked over to Eddie's car had Earl Cooper's blue eyes and his long ears, but there all resemblance stopped. Earl Cooper had walked with a John Wayne strut that pushed forward his massive chest and thick arms and broadcast his power. Matt Cooper held himself with a military posture, but walked easily, like he was calmly strolling down a Wal-Mart aisle.

Eddie rolled down the window. "What seems to be the problem, sheriff?" Eddie was careful to smile and keep his voice neutral although his heart was pounding.

"Please let me see your driver's license and registration, sir."

Well, at least "sir" was a big step-up from the "boy" Eddie was used to as a form of address by white Southerners.

"Here's my license, sir. I need to open the glove compartment to get out the registration. OK?"

"Yes. But keep your hands where I can see them."

Eddie tried to hide his scared expression as he fumbled with finding the registration in the junk-stuffed glove compartment. *Am I going to get shot because that motherfucker Sonny's such a slob?* Eddie wondered. After removing a shriveled apple peel, a crushed soda can, and a pile of scratched-off lottery cards, Eddie finally found the registration and gingerly handed it to the sheriff.

The sheriff scanned the paperwork. "Mr. Baker, this is not your car, is it?"

"No, sir, sheriff. I'm a friend of Sonny Jackson. He's letting me use it while I'm in town."

"And what brings you back to Ruleville? I understand you've been gone a long time," Sheriff Cooper asked as he handed back Eddie's license and Sonny's car registration.

"Just visiting old friends," Eddie said with a big, fake smile. *And visiting old graves*, he thought to himself.

"Well, have a safe visit. Remember, this isn't LA. Ruleville is a peaceful town, and we'd like to keep it that way."

Eddie sat in the car until the sheriff got back into his car and drove off. He lit a cigarette with shaking hands. *See, it's OK.*

Nothin' happened to you, he unsuccessfully tried to convince himself. As Eddie finished his cigarette, a middle-aged white woman came down the path from the farmhouse to the road. She knocked on the passenger's side window. Eddie leaned over and rolled down the window.

"Yes, ma'am?"

"I don't know what you're doing here, but you need to leave my property," the woman said tightly. "Otherwise, I'll get the sheriff back here. I got your license plate number ready to give him," she said, waving a piece of paper.

Hmm, must be some Taylors still around. It's a shame, Eddie thought, the woman would be pretty if it weren't for the deep lines around her mouth and the hateful look in her eyes.

"OK. I was just going," Eddie said. He was parked on a public road, but she didn't look like someone who would appreciate the legal niceties.

As Eddie drove off, he couldn't decide if Sheriff Cooper's parting words were just a typical reaction to someone out of place in the close-knit rural community or a threat. Obviously the next generation of Taylors was as hateful as ever toward black people. That Taylor daughter, or whoever she was, looked like she would just as gladly slit his throat as talk to him. And she seemed confident that the sheriff would back her up in either case.

While retracing her steps to return to the farmhouse, Raelene had a vague sense she had seen that colored boy somewhere before. An uneasy feeling stayed with her as she got ready to go to the White Citizens Council meeting that night.

Although her life had taken some twists and turns, its path seemed to lead directly to the Council. At 17, she had had to drop out of high school to take care of the house and help her father with the farm after her mother was crippled in a car accident. Two years and a lot of pain later, her mother had finally succumbed to her injuries. Raelene resented spending her late teens watching her mother waste away while cooking and cleaning for her increasingly distant father. Raelene looked forward to finally spending time with her friends and looking for a beau. She still had her good looks, even if her hands had roughened from scrubbing dishes. Then her father had started showing signs of Alzheimer's disease. There was no question that she would be chained to him for the foreseeable future. Mercifully, he had gone downhill relatively quickly. When she came back from his funeral to the empty house, she felt just as empty inside. She finally had her freedom, but what to do with it? All she had to her name, besides a somewhat leaky roof over her head, was a farm laden with debt. Her mother, father, and her had worked themselves to the bone all their lives without any help from anyone. It wasn't fair that all those niggas were living on Easy Street, enjoying fat government checks.

The White Citizens Council had taken the place of the much-maligned Klan. It was the more "respectable" face of white pride. When Raelene went to her first meeting, she felt she was with her true family. She recognized some of the men from the old Klan meetings, but there were plenty of new, younger faces too. She was welcomed with open arms.

"Well, if it isn't the daughter of Ray Taylor. I remember you when you was just a mite. Your daddy was a fine man. He'd be so proud you was here," the President told her.

The Council understood why her life seemed out of control. How could it be any different when those damn greedy kikes were running everything! She'd had no idea that Jews controlled the banks, Federal government, and courts. Nobody was standing up for white people. Not only did everything they told her all make sense, but the Council gave her a sense of purpose. Raelene had a remarkable ability to recruit new members. Men liked talking to her, and women didn't feel threatened by her soft approach. She seemed to know exactly what they were feeling. In a couple of years, Raelene had worked her way up to Secretary of the Council. Contacts she made from the Council helped her find a job in a lawyer's office that paid her bills and gave her time off to take care of important Council business. People would be amazed, she often reflected, if they knew how many of their neighbors were secret members of the Council.

She was even dating another devoted member of the Council, Tucker Smith. His rugged good looks and well-toned body were what first attracted her. Knowing he shared her beliefs about white power only deepened the attraction. Plus he was a born-again Christian and true gentleman. He hadn't put the moves on her yet, unlike the men she'd met who couldn't wait to get their hands all over her. Tucker actually thought sex outside marriage was sinful. She had to respect those beliefs. He promised her once he got through a messy custody battle with his ex, he'd be free to marry again. All in all, he seemed worth waiting for.

Tucker was also a self-proclaimed gun nut who talked about firearms with Council members the way other guys talked about baseball. Raelene loved going on walks with him and doing target practice deep in the woods. He wanted her prepared for the racial war that was coming. As a country girl, she could already handle a gun. But now she was becoming a damn good shot, if she did say so herself.

At 8:00, Raelene took her place at the door of a church auditorium used by the Council, greeting people as they arrived for the monthly meeting. They'd originally met in the storeroom of Everett Connors' general store. Once Connors had died from a stroke and the family sold his store, they needed a new place to meet. Besides, they felt the time was right to come out of the shadows. The White Citizens Council deserved a more dignified setting for their noble cause. She had applied for permission to use the auditorium for a "public service group." The church administration had never seemed interested in investigating the use further. Maybe it was because some of the administrators supported the Council's "good Christian works."

After an opening prayer, the Council President gaveled the meeting to order. Two meaty members, Army vets dressed in fatigues, went to stand guard at the door to make sure no nigga-loving troublemakers tried to enter the room. The President, flanked by huge American and Confederate flags, peered over his reading glasses at a sea of eager faces.

"Tonight we ain't discussing the upcoming race war or the disgusting rise in interracial marriage. Tonight we're facing a bigger threat, the persecution of Earl Cooper."

"Damn right it's persecution," someone yelled. "They should be going after all the kike thieves and nigga thugs instead of an upstanding white man like Earl Cooper."

"I wish we could put up a statue honoring Earl Cooper," one woman said indignantly. "He's a hero, that's what he is."

"Even worse, the case hinges on the word of a turncoat, Rusty Miller," the President continued. "He's a traitor to our race."

"I'd donate money to build a statue of anyone who shot that motherfucker Rusty Miller," a well-respected local businessman added. "Sorry for my language, ladies. But the shooter would be the real hero."

That got a huge round of applause. In the end, they decided to organize a march outside the courthouse and leaflet as many cars as they could. To some members, it wasn't nearly enough to protest the gross miscarriage of justice taking place inside the courthouse.

Raelene hadn't really thought about the lynching she had seen for years. But now, as she thought about Earl Cooper, she could see the details of that night in her mind as if it were yesterday. Wait! So that was what was bothering her. That man she had seen parked by the farm, he *could* be the teenager she had seen leave the barn. He had the same Jap-looking eyebrows. She hadn't ever told anyone what she saw, not even Tucker. She was afraid he'd condemn her for not reporting that nigga boy to her father. But now was her chance to make sure that boy couldn't cause trouble. First, she'd have to do some research to make sure it was the same boy, eyebrows or not. She was glad she had kept his license number.

"Raelene, darlin', are you with us? You look a little lost," Tucker asked.

"I'm sorry. Yes, I'm definitely here and eager to go."

As soon as she got to work the next morning, she called the sheriff's office and spoke to a Council member who worked there.

"Morning, sugar," Raelene purred. "Can you do me a small favor? It's for the cause."

"Anything to help."

"Can you run this license plate number for me?"

"Sure."

He was repeating the number when Raelene heard a voice asking him a question in the background.

"Gotta go," he whispered. "Let me call you back with that info, ma'am," he said loudly before hanging up.

He called back and told her the plates were registered to Sonny Jackson. He helpfully gave her the addresses of Sonny's house and business for good measure.

"How long's this Sonny been around?"

"Oh, a good long while. But I did hear that this boy, Eddie Baker, is back in town from California and staying with the Jacksons."

"When did this Eddie go away?"

She waited while he did the math in his head.

"As best I can figure it, he's been gone some 30 years. I do believe he's the one who hightailed it out of town after they found Bertie Lambert's body. I don't keep track of the coloreds' comings and goings that much. Why? Is he causing trouble? Maybe I can help."

"I can't go into details, but it's better you stay out of this particular piece of business. But you were real helpful and I'll be sure the rest of the Council officials know about it. Oh, one more thing. Call me right away if that Eddie Baker shows up in the sheriff's office for any reason."

"Will do."

Raelene looked at the pile of work on her desk. This Eddie problem could probably keep until that night. She'd rather take care of business at night anyway. No sense in getting sloppy and drawing attention to herself, no matter how righteous her acts.

**CHAPTER 13**

Eddie had tried not to get his hopes up, but as he approached the area where his and Rosalynn's "meeting shack" used to stand in a bend by the river, all he saw was an empty patch of ground. Not only wasn't her car there, but there was no longer any trace of the shack. It had just been a primitive shelter for fishermen. A flood must have finally taken it away. As he sat reminiscing about the good times Rosalynn and he had shared in that shack, he heard a car approaching.

He walked over to the car as Rosalynn got out. Her stony expression was a sharp contrast to the laughing, carefree teenager he had been thinking about.

"Thanks a lot for coming, Rosalynn," he said sincerely. "I wasn't sure if you'd show up."

"I did it for EJ, not for you. Yes, he's your blood. I'll give you that. I was pregnant when you left. That's what I wanted to talk to you about that night, if you'd shown up. You probably knew I was pregnant and lit out the first chance you got."

"So it's true. I'm EJ's father." Eddie had been grappling with the possibility since Sonny had told him the timeframe around EJ's birth. Now he couldn't deny it anymore. He wasn't sure if the twisted feeling in his gut was apprehension or elation. Maybe it was a little of both. He was so used to feeling bad about his life, it was hard to accept he had earned any rewards for his actions.

"I swear I didn't know you were pregnant. But you have to trust me, Rosalynn, I had a good reason to leave when I did."

"Last time you told me to trust you was when you told me it was okay to lay together because we'd be getting married."

"I was a selfish boy then. I'm a man now, ready to accept my responsibilities."

"You think you can just waltz in here and be EJ's father? A real father is there for his son. You used to feel sorry for yourself because your father walked out on you. Well, you're just like him!" she sneered. "You've never been there for EJ and it's way too late to start now. He don't need you or want you."

Her words pierced him to his core. Eddie turned his head toward the river so she wouldn't see his pain. "I forgot how peaceful it is down here," he said softly. Eddie took a deep breath and savored the cool smell of the river. They stood side by side, together but apart, absorbing the quiet, which was interrupted only by the buzzing of mosquitos and the occasional splashing of a fish. He grabbed a leaf off a bush and twisted the stem around and around in his hands.

"I can't imagine how you felt that night, or all the nights after that. I want ya to know that it killed me not to say good-bye, but I did it to protect you."

"Protect me? How was your leaving protecting me? Everybody was afraid of the Klan, especially after Bertie's body was found. But we didn't all run out with our tails between our legs. Be honest, you left because you were just a big, fat coward."

"Do you really hate me that much?"

"I don't hate you. I certainly don't love you. Don't you get it? You're nothing to me. A ghost. A figment of my imagination."

Eddie's body felt so heavy he wouldn't have been surprised if he had sunk straight down into the soft Mississippi soil without a trace.

"Rosalynn, you're the only person on the Lord's green earth I'm telling this. I didn't leave because I was scared after Bertie was killed that the Klan was coming after all black men. I was scared because I knew what happened to Bertie. I knew because I saw Bertie get killed."

"Are you telling me you were actually there when it happened?" Eddie nodded.

"Yeah, right. Why would they kill Bertie and let you go scot-free?"

"You remember how it started storming that night?"

"How can I forget? I was sitting alone in that raggedy-ass shack when buckets of rain came down, pouring through the leaks in that excuse of a roof. With all the thunderin' and lightnin', I thought that old shack would blow right into the river. Where were you?"

Eddie's words came pouring out. "When the storm came on, I took shelter in Ray Taylor's barn. I heard white voices outside, so I run up into the hayloft. They never saw me. I could see everything that happened through a knothole in the floor of the loft. Ray, Everett Connors, the sheriff, and two redheads brought Bertie in. He had a hood on, but I knew it was him. He could barely walk, and his arms were a mass of bruises. Then they hung him, right there in the barn. After they took his dead body down and left, I started running. And I haven't really stopped running since."

There, he had said it. Eddie looked straight down at the ground. He couldn't bear to see the expression on Rosalynn's face. He didn't know what reaction he expected. Sympathy? Disgust? Forgiveness? Hate? It didn't matter. Any reaction would mean she saw him as a flesh-and-blood human being again.

Rosalynn was silent for what seemed an eternity. Then she finally asked, "So you saying you only came back because of the trial? You think you're home-free now?"

"Sonny was the one who convinced me to come back," Eddie said. "I'll never be home-free, no matter what happens with the trial," he added emphatically.

"Ya know they got Rusty Miller to testify, heard they made some kind of deal with him. That must be one of the redheads you saw. His brother Wade is long dead. If something happened to Rusty, you'd be the only thing standing between Sheriff Cooper's freedom and justice *finally* for Bertie's family. What would you do then?"

"I honestly don't know, Rosalynn. There ain't a night that goes by that I haven't thought about Bertie. Drinking hasn't helped. I sure tried to drown out what I saw with rivers of whiskey. Women haven't helped. Sure, I had fun, but I couldn't let any of them get close and know what a coward I really was. Playing my guitar and singing the blues is the only thing that has kept me going all these years. The possibility that I have a son, that my life hasn't all been in vain . . ." He got too choked up to say anything else.

Rosalynn took his arm and turned him around so he was looking right into her eyes. "I might not have always been the best mother, but I've always been honest with EJ. I didn't see no sense in makin' up stories about his father. Momma and Alma knew about you anyway. Alma warned me about gettin' too serious with you, but I didn't pay her no mind. I'll leave it up to EJ if he wants to talk to you. He's a grown man and can make his own decisions. I figured sooner or later someone would tell him you're in town and he might be curious to talk to you. I can't stop him, although I think nothin' good will come of it. But EJ must never know you saw that murder. I don't want him drawn into that mess. Also, you can't be askin' him to go visit you in Los Angeles. I need him down here with me. Do you promise me, Eddie? Do you swear on your aunt and uncle's graves?"

"I promise," Eddie said solemnly.

Rosalynn took a slip of paper out of her purse and wrote down EJ's address. "He don't live with me. He lives with his fiancée. He works as a plumber's apprentice, but he don't have set hours. When do you think you'll go see him?"

"I'll try to see him the day after tomorrow. Tomorrow night the old crew—you know, Sonny, Skeeter, and Luther—and me are getting together to play some music. You're welcome to join us. I know you always liked my guitar playing. It's gotten a lot better," he couldn't help adding.

"I don't think so, Eddie. Whatever happened between us back then is long gone and it ain't ever coming back." She got into her car and drove off. He stood watching until the last glow from her car's taillights faded from the road.

CHAPTER 14

**When Eddie returned,** Sonny was frantically pacing up and down the living room floor, with occasional stops to take a quick peek out the side of the closed curtains. Eddie had never seen his good-natured friend in such a frenzied state.

"Thank the Lord you're back. There's been some goddamned skinhead looking for you. Of course we didn't tell him you're staying here. What's this all about? He sure as hell ain't from around here; he had some kind of Northern accent. We're going to have to keep you hidden in case he returns with the rest of his gang."

Eddie started to take a peek out the window.

"Stay away from the window," Sonny begged.

"What did this guy look like?"

"He's a huge motherfucker, about 6'4" tall, shaved head, tattoos everywhere not covered by black leather. He came roaring in on a Harley. What he looks like is trouble, with a capital T. I was ready to grab the baseball bat behind the door when he left."

Sonny's jaw dropped when his friend started roaring with laughter.

"That's my friend Nick from LA. He's no more a skinhead than you are," Eddie managed to say between paroxysms of laughter. "Do you know where he went?"

"I have no idea, but he shouldn't be too hard to spot in this town."

Eddie thought about it for a minute. After his frustrating encounter with Sonny, Nick was probably sulking and having a drink somewhere. The most likely spot was a white watering hole Eddie knew only by reputation near the tracks that usually had a motorcycle or two parked outside.

"I'm goin' lookin' for him. I *think* I know where he is."

"Good luck. It sounds like you'll need it."

Eddie cautiously pulled into the lot of the Ruleville Roadhouse, ready to make a quick getaway if Nick wasn't there. But sure enough, he saw Nick's familiar Harley parked near a row of dusty trucks flaunting Confederate flag window decals. Eddie was not thrilled about going into a white bar, but he figured Nick would have his back no matter what.

Eddie walked in with his head held high, trying to exude the confidence he didn't have. He felt the glare of the bar patrons burning into the back of his neck as he passed them. Two of them stopped a conversation in mid-sentence to swivel around and silently glower at him. The Allman Brothers' version of *One Way Out* was blaring out of the jukebox.

I wonder what would happen if I told these good ole boys they're really listening to black music seeing as this song was written by Sonny Boy Williamson. Naw, not a good move. It would probably turn into *No Way Out* for my black ass.

Eddie let out a deep sigh of relief when he spotted Nick in the dim, smoke-filled interior. Nick was by himself at the end of the bar. Even the local rednecks were giving him a wide berth. Nick had his back to him, pretending to be engrossed in a NASCAR race on TV.

Eddie kept his eyes on some pool players as he dropped into

the barstool next to his friend. They stood up from the pool table and threateningly gripped their cue sticks as they stared at him. He better make this quick.

"Hi there, big guy. Come here often?" Eddie whispered into Nick's ear in a feminine falsetto.

Nick swiveled around and broke into a big smile when he saw Eddie.

"Hell no. This is my first and definitely last time in this piss-poor excuse of a city. At least the beer is cheap."

"So, what are you doing here? Don't tell me you missed me already."

"It was Sylvia that missed you. She thinks something's wrong you didn't tell her about. She begged me to go to Mississippi and watch your back."

"I know you, Nick. What else is going on?"

"Remember that redhead I told you about?"

He nodded. Eddie normally would need a scorecard to keep track of Nick's conquests, but he remembered her from their talk on their way back from the Piazzas'.

"It turns out her husband's a cop, and he wasn't too thrilled to find out about me. As a matter of fact, he threatened to shoot my ass if he caught me sniffing around his wife. I figured getting out of LA and calming down Sylvia by visiting you would be a win-win."

"Uh-huh. And that's all it took for you to ride all the way cross-country?"

Nick picked at the edges of his beer bottle's label. "Alright, but don't laugh. I wanted to experience the true heart and soul of the blues, ya know, the real shit, here in the Delta where it all started. You always talked about what an amazing player Otha was. I'd like to hear a guy like that play genuine country blues. I figured this was my chance."

"I wish I could hear Otha play again, too. Sorry, Nick, most of them old-timers are gone or ain't playing anymore. You'll have to settle for hearing me and my friends play. You planning on stickin' 'round for a while?"

"I'm in no rush to go back."

"What did you do with that mutt of yours?"

"Chester's staying with Laura. He's in good hands."

Laura was an ex-girlfriend who probably loved Chester more than she ever did Nick. She didn't have a clue, though, that Chester the dog had been named in honor of Chester Arthur Burnett, aka Howlin' Wolf.

Nick waved one of his big paws to get the attention of the bartender to bring over a drink for Eddie, but the bartender pointedly ignored him. Eddie saw the flush of anger spreading from the top of Nick's head and the veins in his neck starting to pulse. Uh-oh, he knew where this was heading. It wouldn't matter to Nick that they were outnumbered seven to two. By standing up for Eddie, he'd probably get them both killed.

"Don't, Nick," Eddie said, gripping his friend's beefy arm. "He really ain't worth it. Let's go back and try it again with Sonny. You know, he's a huge Little Walter fan too. That should help smooth things over. His wife Pearline loves a big-time eater. She'll be in hog heaven when she gets a load of your appetite."

"Well, I *am* hungry," Nick said reluctantly. "Maybe I'll stop by for some grub before I head out to the campsite I rented. I already set up my camping gear."

"And exactly when *aren't* you hungry?" Eddie replied. That at least got Nick to smile. "Let's get the hell out of here."

When they walked outside and hit the evening's lingering heat, Eddie realized he had been shivering. This may be the new South, but nobody seemed to have told the guys in the bar that.

Raelene had followed Eddie from Sonny's house. You could have knocked her over with a feather when she saw Eddie drive over to the Ruleville Roadhouse, let alone enter it. He had balls, she had to give him that. Maybe the good ole boys inside would take care of her problem for her. Even if she marched in and shot Eddie at point-blank range, she was confident there wouldn't be anyone inside willing to testify against her. She wasn't sure about that white giant. When she had first spotted him roaring in by motorcycle as she staked out Sonny's house, she thought he must be a brother-in-arms with his own grudge against Eddie. Now after seeing the way they acted together, she realized he was the worst kind of traitor, a nigga-lover through and through. She'd have to pick a better time and place. No sense pushing her luck.

Although she was loath to share all the glory of saving Earl Cooper by eliminating this possible witness against him, Raelene decided she better call in some reinforcements. There was only one person she could rely on. She called him as soon as she got back to the office.

"Hello, Tucker. We gotta talk."

"What's the matter, honey?"

"Do you think you could come over to my house? I'll be home in another hour."

"You bet."

Raelene not only liked Tucker, she trusted him. He'd come clean on their first date that he'd recently gotten out of prison.

"Some nigga jumped me in a bar in Greenville, so I cut him. It was self-defense, but of course I was the one who had to do the time," he told her.

It was while he was in prison that his wife left him. He was in his darkest despair when he found Jesus. He'd found further salvation when he came across the writings of the Council. They'd even explained how Scripture supported white supremacy.

"Well, amen to that!"

"My record's made it hard for me to get any kind of real job, though."

She clicked her tongue in sympathy. "Ain't it always the way. So what do you do to keep body and soul together?"

Raelene didn't want to come across as some kind of money grubber, but she didn't want to get involved with someone who couldn't cut it either. She was tired of taking care of herself.

"Oh, I do some odds and ends with my cousin," he said vaguely. "Plus I got some savings my ex can't get her hands on," he added with a smile. "But don't you worry your pretty head about it. I know how to treat a woman right."

And he had proven to be as good as his word. He seemed to have enough money to treat Raelene to nice meals. He spoiled her with flowers and boxes of candy. She sometimes worried that the "odds and ends" with his cousin involved drug dealing. It would explain the money. He seemed paranoid about being around any law enforcement. But she wasn't sure how a born-again Christian could be involved in selling drugs. She'd never even seen him drink more than two beers. Maybe it was better she didn't really know.

He greeted her at her house with a light kiss.

"I'm here for you, baby. What's on your mind?"

"Sit down and make yourself comfortable. I'll be right back."

Raelene returned with a couple of cold beers.

He waited patiently while they both took some long swallows.

"Tucker, I never told you this before, but I saw the lynching of that trouble-making Yankee nigga when I was 11. It took place right here, in our barn. I had snuck in to see it. It was Earl Cooper, Everett Connors, the Miller brothers, and my daddy who done it."

She waited for his reaction.

"Well, you must be right proud of your daddy," he said with a big grin. "Why do you sound so worried?"

"After the lynching and everybody had left, I saw some nigga boy come down from the hayloft and take off. He musta been there the whole time. Nobody else saw him. I didn't tell my daddy 'cause I'd of been in a world of trouble just for being there."

"I can understand that."

"And that boy never said nothing to nobody. Matter of fact, I found out he hightailed it out of town as soon as he could. But now I could swear I seen him back in town. I'm afraid he's here to testify at Earl's trial. We gotta do something!"

"What did you have in mind?"

"What do you think? He needs his big nigga lips shut, *permanently*. I know where he lives."

Tucker looked thoughtful. "If he was that much of a coward to take off like that, don't you think we could just scare him off again? I've been in prison. I don't wanna ever go back. But even more importantly, I couldn't bear to see you go to prison," he said earnestedly, taking her hand.

Raelene tried to hide her disappointment. Tucker wasn't the man she thought he was. It looked like she'd never find anybody who could measure up to her daddy.

"OK, Tucker. We'll try it your way. But we can't get other Council members involved. I don't want them all to know I coulda gotten this taken care of 30 years ago."

"Leave it to me, honey. Just give me that boy's name and address."

Raelene wrote the information on a slip of paper and handed it to him.

"How'd you track him down anyway?"

"Wouldn't you like to know," she answered playfully. "You'd be surprised what a Southern woman can do once she puts her mind to it."

Tucker raised his beer bottle in a toast. "Here's to Southern women."

"You wanna stay for dinner? I'm dying to hear what you're gonna do."

"I wish I could. I wanna get started on takin' care of this, um, problem right away. It'll be safer for you not to know the details. I'm just lookin' out for you, darlin'."

After Tucker left and Raelene thought about what he had said, she got angrier and angrier. There wasn't time to sit around on their asses and see if that boy could be scared off. She knew what her daddy would do and she was gonna do it! She owed it to his memory.

And if Tucker wasn't going to help her with this, she wasn't about to talk to him about other plans she had. This Southern woman was going to take matters into her own hands.

CHAPTER 15

The Sunflower County DA's Department was keeping Rusty Miller under wraps in a rundown motel offering cheap day rates on I-55, on the outskirts of Jackson. It had the double advantage of being easy on the DA's budget while providing anonymity from the prying eyes of Ruleville.

Although his trademark red hair had receded over the years, the scraggly patch that survived along the back of his skull and his bushy eyebrows still bore witness to his nickname. His past addiction to meth had aged him way past his 52 years. When he was arrested for intent to distribute for the second time, he was facing a lifetime behind bars. He only had one thing left to trade and that was the murder of Bertie Johnson. His brother Wade was dead, so they couldn't touch him. Rusty still believed passionately in the superiority of whites and felt justified keeping the "mongrel races" in line by any means possible. His many years in prison surrounded by the Aryan Brotherhood had only reinforced those beliefs. But his main loyalty was to himself, so he had no problem selling out Earl Cooper. He was just anxious for the trial to be over.

He might be a dead man after he testified, but he had been a dead man walking the past 3 years anyway.

The police detail protecting him, including Officer Thompson, a young black man, were not particularly worried about Rusty's safety. This was a 30-year-old case that had been cold a long time, even though it was stirring up some hot passions now. Most people directly connected to the case had died. The once seemingly invincible Klan's hold over the South had at last been breached with the successful conviction of Byron de la Beckwith for the killing of Medgar Evers. Thompson knew Rusty's background, but he was a professional who kept his personal feelings toward prisoners in check. To Thompson, Rusty was a meek shadow of a man who didn't even have it in him to squawk about the saggy bed or monotonous fast-food diet. He never tried to draw Thompson into personal conversation, which suited him fine, even if it made the time drag.

There was no fear that Rusty would try to escape police custody. It was in Rusty's best interest to testify. Thompson knew it broke protocol, but he decided to leave the room to get a pack of cigarettes from the motel lobby instead of waiting for the nighttime backup to arrive. He would only be gone 5 minutes, tops. The prisoner had one arm handcuffed to a chair. When he left, carefully locking the door, Rusty was contentedly gnawing on a drumstick from a bucket of Kentucky Fried Chicken and watching some barely clothed dancers on MTV. He just grunted when Thompson said he would be right back.

Thompson never heard the gunshot over the roar of traffic and the blaring TV in the motel's lobby. He came back to find Rusty sprawled out on the floor, dead from a single shot that had obviously been fired through the partially opened window. Thompson called for backup and they canvassed all the rooms. The hookers who reluctantly opened the doors, and then only after making sure their johns were out of sight, said they hadn't seen or heard anything. The one harassed housekeeper said she was in the laundry room. Whoever had shot him was long gone.

After Officer Thompson was disciplined for leaving the prisoner alone, the ball was back in the DA's court to find another way to prosecute the Cooper case.

CHAPTER 16

**Sonny had** arranged for the old music-making gang to reunite that night. Eddie was looking forward to hooking up with the gang, but first he had to make one important stop by himself to connect with other important people from his past. The cemetery of the Mt. Zion Baptist Church was a refuge of flowering dogwood trees, simple tombstones, and pieces of Eddie's heart.

He placed a small bouquet of flowers on his mother's grave. "Sorry, momma, for not visiting you more. I wish ya could see me play. I think you'd be proud of me."

Right next to her were his aunt and uncle's graves. The church's windows were open, and Eddie could hear the voices of the choir practice floating over the cemetery. He smiled, knowing his mother and aunt would eternally be within hearing distance of their beloved church music.

"Hello, old friend," Eddie said kneeling at Otha's grave. At least Otha was where he wanted to be, finally reunited with his beloved Lucy Anne.

Otha might have been his friend, grandpop, father confessor, and more, but it was hard to call him "teacher." Otha didn't follow the traditional role of a teacher showing a student what to do. Maybe "truth shower" would be a better label. Otha would play something and say, "Here it is." According to Otha, if you get it, you supposed to. If you don't, the hell with you!

Eddie would ask what tuning he was in. Otha pointed to the tuning pegs as he went along: "This go down, this go down, this the same, this the same, this the same, this go down, and you dere." He'd flash Eddie a big grin to make sure Eddie was in on the joke.

Otha taught him a helluva lot more than guitar "technique." When Eddie played too many notes for Otha's taste, he'd say, "Look son, when in doubt, leave it out." That stayed with Eddie all through his career. It was why so many of the LA blues musicians liked him as a player—he knew how to use space. Otha taught him that space is music too.

Eddie wiped away a few tears. Otha would consider crying at someone's grave a waste of time. It wasn't going to bring anyone back. Now sharing some timeless blues, *that* Otha would appreciate. Eddie softly sang Blind Lemon Jefferson's *Please See That My Grave Is Kept Clean* as he pulled out a couple of weeds sprouting near the grave. Eddie rose off his knees and quietly said, "Thank you, Mr. Otha," before leaving the cemetery. He never noticed the woman intently watching him from the car parked across from the cemetery.

The sober mood that hung over him at the cemetery evaporated as he thought about playing that evening. Yes, life was short, but good music and good friends made it all worthwhile. They were getting together in Sonny's auto shop, bad acoustics and all. At least with the front bay doors open, there would be a pleasant breeze. Truth be told, there was no place else for the four old friends to get together and play. Pearline had put her foot down over a reunion at Sonny's house. She knew he listened to the "Devil's music" when she wasn't around, but she drew the line at a live concert in her backyard. Besides, how could they play somewhere they couldn't even drink?

Eddie *had* hoped they could play at DeeDee's Lounge, about 5 miles away from Ruleville proper. Sadly, it had gone the way of many Southern juke joints. The old-time regulars had died off and newer generations, hooked on hip-hop, could care less about the blues. Sonny took him on a trip there for old time's sake, before they were due at his garage.

Peering into DeeDee's dusty windows was like viewing a world that time forgot. The place was still held together in spots with baling wire and decorated with Christmas lights that no longer twinkled. Maybe the vinyl tops of the bar stools had more duct tape than Eddie remembered. It still felt more like home to Eddie than anyplace in Ruleville. Sure, Front Street, better known as Greasy Street, had once been the spot in Ruleville for all kinds of swinging music. In its heyday, great blues musicians such as Charley Patton, David "Honeyboy" Edwards, and Howlin' Wolf had played at places like Mack's Colored Cafe. The clubs had slowly winked out, like dying embers from a once blazing fire. The country juke joints hadn't fared much better.

Eddie and their little group had played for other friends and even at a couple of high school events, but DeeDee's held a special place in his heart. It was where he had first played before a live audience for tips. Even if the audience had paid more attention to their drinks and partners than his playing, he felt excited to be on a stage that had hosted famous musicians like Sonny Boy Williamson II and Honeyboy Edwards. When their bands had played, the joint was filled with sweaty couples dancing 'til the music or their legs gave out. It was the place for hip-grinding hot blues and ice cold beers. Eddie had to leave Saturday nights before the action really got going because his aunt would wake him up bright and early for church services. Knowing Sunday morning meant getting up with the roosters didn't stop some folks from staying up all night "witnessing" at their favorite blues joint and then going straight to the Baptist church for a different type of soul rousing. These were the bleary-eyed souls, wincing from hangovers, that the preacher focused on during his fiery anti-drinking sermons.

DeeDee had been one tough lady. She didn't hesitate to throw out especially rowdy customers or bluesmen that couldn't keep the joint jumping. Eddie was amazed to watch her once sweet-talk a drunk who thought someone was giving his woman too much attention. She got him to put down his knife and join her for a drink.

After DeeDee died and her customers either emigrated up North or died off, a few hard-core regulars kept coming to share memories and cheap drinks. No matter how hard he tried, her son Junior just couldn't afford to keep it going. Tourists showed up now and then, many of them from Europe or Japan, if they could decipher the vague directions to its location. The tourists satisfied themselves with a few pictures of the one-room shack with its hand-painted sign and sagging porch before driving off.

It wasn't a tourist, however, who was sitting in a car across the road from DeeDee's. Raelene had followed Sonny and Eddie there. Even though they were out in the country, anyone could see the parking lot from the road. She was disappointed but knew she must be patient. It would be worth it for her to bide her time. When their car left and headed back toward town, Raelene followed closely behind them. She didn't notice a car pull out from a side road and follow several car lengths behind her. She didn't notice because that driver was well trained in surveillance. If he didn't want to be observed, he wouldn't be. Sonny and Eddie weren't aware of any of this attention. They were busy sharing stories about some of DeeDee's more colorful patrons.

"I miss playing at DeeDee's," Eddie told Sonny as they arrived at his garage. "The clubs in LA are great, man, but ain't nothing like a downhome juke joint to get the juices going."

"Well tonight we all are gonna make sure those greasy blues are alive and well. We're so fucking excited to play with ya and see what ya got. You gotta appreciate that."

"Yeah, you got that right. I bet you cats are gonna give me a run for my money."

Eddie was still going to miss the energy that radiates from an audience. At least he'd have other musicians to jam with. Usually the give-and-take on stage pushed him to his best playing.

"Now that's what I'm talking about," Eddie exclaimed, slapping the hands of Luther and Skeeter as he entered the garage. Sonny trailed behind him, beaming like a proud papa.

"I about fell out when Sonny told us you were back in town," Skeeter said.

"Sheeet," Luther joined in, "if you ain't a sight for sore eyes."

With Luther on bass, Skeeter on drums, Eddie playing guitar, and Sonny on harp, they hadn't sounded half bad, even as teenagers. Different people had dropped in and out of their group, but they had always liked playing with each other the most. They felt like brothers of another mother before that phrase became popular.

At first glance it was hard to believe Luther and Skeeter were actual brothers, let alone fraternal twins. Luther was 6' tall and rail thin. He still wore a pencil-thin mustache that looked like it hadn't added a hair since his teenage days. While the other kids had run around in a perpetual cloud of dust, Luther had liked to keep himself church-day clean. As manager of a boutique men's store in Jackson, he took advantage of his role and dressed to the nines—even when he wasn't working. Luther showed up wearing a light blue seersucker suit with matching paisley tie and handkerchief. Skeeter was average height and weight, but he had always looked small compared to his older (by five minutes) brother. His real name was Lester, but nobody had called him that since his grandmother took one look at him when the premature twins came home from the hospital and declared, "Why he ain't any bigger than a skeeter bite." Eddie secretly thought the nickname stuck because Skeeter's constant complaining sounded like the whine of buzzing insect wings.

"It's been a while, man," Eddie said, surveying his eager bandmates. "Hmm, let's do *Smokestack Lightning*, the old Wolf song."

"That's cool. We all know that riff and it's only got one chord!" Luther said.

They all laughed. If they had been self-conscious about playing with Eddie, they weren't now.

Skeeter set the tempo with his sticks. Eddie hit the well-known riff. Sonny and Skeeter joined him after four bars.

With the first notes, they felt like they had played just yesterday instead of over 30 years ago. Eddie was enthusiastically playing and singing when the drums and bass suddenly stopped mid-note. Eddie followed his friends' astonished stares to see Nick climb off his Harley and confidently walk over to them.

"I know, she's a real beauty, ain't she," Nick said, assuming they were staring at the custom chrome work on his bike. "How ya doing? Don't stop playing on my account, Eddie."

"Who the hell is this, your bodyguard?" Skeeter asked. "I don't see crowds of anxious fans trying to get a piece of you."

"This here's my friend Nick from LA. I guess Sonny forgot to tell you he was coming. He's good people."

"Any friends of Eddie's are friends of mine," Nick proclaimed, vigorously pumping each of the brothers' hands. "Man, I've heard so much about your playing together. Don't let me stop you fellas; that was a serious groove you had working on *Smokestack Lightning*."

He pulled up a rickety swivel chair, carefully placing his huge bulk on the edge so he wouldn't fall over.

"Guys, play loud," Eddie exhorted his bandmates. "We need to drown Nick out if he tries to sing."

Drawn by the strands of music wafting over the warm night's

air, passers-by stopped to check it out. Soon they had a small, but appreciative, impromptu audience.

All that playing made them thirsty. Skeeter had provided a cooler packed with beers. After playing *I Don't Want No Woman*, courtesy of Magic Sam, and the B.B. King classic, *How Blue Can You Get*, they paused to take some long swallows. Eddie got ready to light up a cigarette.

"Can't you read?" Sonny yelled, pointing to a "No Smoking" sign.

"What are you talking about?"

"There's too many gas and oil spills around the bays. If you want to smoke, you gotta go around back."

"Sorry, folks, we gotta take a pause for the cause. We'll be back later," Eddie promised. The handful of listeners they had attracted drifted off.

The small band of friends flopped down on a couple of seats salvaged from an ancient Caddy. Sonny pulled out a bottle of Wild Turkey that had been hidden under the seats.

"See, all the comforts of home," Sonny said, waving his arm around the junkyard of rusting cars while taking a swig of whiskey. "And without the yammering of certain others at home."

"Well, if we have to smoke back here, we might as well make the most of it." Nick pulled a joint out of his pack of Marlboros, took a long drag, and held it out to Skeeter. Skeeter hesitated.

"C'mon. Nick's not trying to poison you," Eddie assured him. "Trust me, he always has some good shit."

"Well, if you ain't gonna take it, that leaves all the more for us," Luther said, reaching for the joint. "Since when does someone have to twist your arm to share a joint?"

Luther took a drag. In between coughs, he said, "Yeah, that's some good shit." He passed it over to Skeeter's outreached hand. They finished off the joint and cooled off their mouths with the rest of the whiskey bottle.

"OK. I'm *really* ready to play some bad-ass blues now," Sonny said, staggering to his feet.

"Yeah, but first I gotta take a leak. Where's the bathroom, Sonny?" Eddie asked.

"Back there," Sonny replied, jerking his thumb toward a clump of bushes and a scraggly looking magnolia tree. "Sorry, the inside one's out of order and I ain't gotten around to fixing it."

"We'll meet you back inside in a minute. Mustn't keep our devoted fans waiting."

"Good idea. I'm coming with you buddy," Nick said. He helped Eddie to his unsteady feet and guided him toward the bushes to do their business.

Nick reacted first to the unmistakable blast of a shotgun. He tackled Eddie to the ground just as a second shell whizzed past.

"What the fuck?" Eddie yelled through a mouthful of dirt.

"Stay down," Nick shouted.

Sonny and Luther came running from the inside of the garage. When Eddie scrambled to his feet, he saw the gash in the tree left by the second shotgun blast right where he had been standing. If Nick hadn't pushed him away, Eddie would be getting ready to jam with some of his favorite departed blues heroes. Guess his dream gig with Charley Patton, Lightnin' Hopkins, Otis Spann, and Little Walter would thankfully be put off.

Skeeter sheepishly crawled out from some bushes.

"What are you doing back there?" Luther demanded.

"Looking for my contact lenses," he said sarcastically. "What do you think I was doing? When I heard the blast, I dove into the bushes."

"Did you see anybody?" Eddie asked.

"No. I thought I heard someone run past me that way," he pointed.

A flashlight pointed at their eyes, temporarily blinding them.

"This is Sheriff Cooper," a voice behind the flashlight boomed. "Put your hands up."

The five men raised their hands.

"Okay, now over to the building, up against the wall."

"Why are you treating us like criminals? We're the ones who were being shot at," Nick angrily said, pointing to the bullet lodged in the tree.

"It's okay, Nick. The man's just doing his job." How could Eddie explain to him that black men couldn't challenge any law enforcement. That confronting the sheriff could be more detrimental to their health than a shooter who obviously had bad aim.

Eddie, Luther, Skeeter, and Sonny turned around and put their hands against the wall. Sheriff Cooper methodically patted each of them down. Nick stood with his arms folded, glaring at the sheriff.

"Ya like being with the brothers but you still think that white skin makes you special," Skeeter yelled at Nick. "You gotta pay up. We in the shit; you in the shit."

Nick slowly turned around and let the sheriff search him. The sheriff pulled a knife out of Nick's boot but handed it back.

"Yeah, that white boy is special," Skeeter muttered under his breath.

"I was on patrol and heard some gunshots," the sheriff said. "Was anybody hurt?"

Luther and Sonny started excitedly talking over each other.

"Hold up," he said.

The sheriff pointed at Eddie. "You're bleeding, Mr. Baker."

Eddie looked down to see a trickle of blood oozing out of his left arm. He had thought the stab of pain he was feeling might have been caused by a sharp rock when he hit the ground. Now he realized he had been nicked by a shell.

"Let me look at it."

The sheriff focused the flashlight on Eddie's arm.

"It's just a flesh wound, but you're going to need a doctor to look at it."

Eddie flexed his fingers. "I can still play. That's all I care about."

Sheriff Cooper spoke into his radio and within a few minutes, another car arrived and discharged a pair of deputy sheriffs.

A new audience had gathered, attracted not by music but by the sheriff cars' flashing lights.

"OK, folks, show's over. Go on home."

"You guys can go too, but not until you each give a statement to Officer Gregory."

"Officer Armes, sweep the area for evidence and see if there are any other witnesses."

"Damn, what a motherfucking way to end the night," said Luther. "And we were just getting warmed up."

"Don't think I'm done with you," the sheriff said, pointing at Eddie. "If someone was trying to shoot you, we need to have a private conversation. I'll let you go now to get that wound taken care of, but I expect you in my office first thing in the morning. Alone," he said, staring at Nick.

Even in the dark, Eddie could see his friend tensing up.

"Sonny, why don't you head back home. Nick will give me a ride back."

"Is that OK, Nick? I'll try not to bleed all over your bike."

"You'd better not. Here," said Nick, holding out a handkerchief, "press this against your arm."

They got about halfway back when the weight of what had happened hit Eddie like a sucker punch. Eddie tugged on his friend's arm to stop. He got off the bike, slid up the helmet, and threw up on the side of the road.

"Feel better?"

Eddie nodded.

"Good. And I appreciate you doing that away from my bike."

When they pulled up to Sonny's house, Sonny was pacing up and down the front porch.

Eddie slid off the bike. Nick helped Eddie take off his helmet so he wouldn't have to take his hand off the handkerchief, which was drenched in blood.

"Thanks, man. Don't worry. I'll get this washed before I return it."

"I got bigger things to worry about. Like, why the fuck was somebody shooting at you? You just got here. It doesn't seem like you'd have enough time to piss off anybody. And while we're at it, why exactly are you down here? I know Sonny called you, someone you haven't been in touch with for 30 years. I never once heard you say you missed Mississippi and wished you could visit. And you hate traveling, even for good gigs. Yet you dropped everything and hightailed your ass down here. What the hell is going on?"

"Nick, I appreciate your concern. I really do. It's not something I can talk about right now. And honestly, I have no idea why someone was shooting at me. Just promise not to tell Sylvia about it."

"I'll think about it," Nick said, revving up his Harley.

"Thanks, man, for *everything*. I owe you one."

Pearline was waiting for him when Sonny opened the door. Eddie suddenly felt bone tired, too tired to stop Pearline from marching him right into the bathroom so she could take care of the wound.

"Don't worry, baby. I got three children, so I'm used to having to patch up their messes."

Eddie bit his tongue hard to avoid letting out a string of curses as she poured some peroxide over it.

"It don't look like you need stitches. I'd still let a doctor look at it," she said, wrapping a dressing around it. "We got a decent clinic hereabouts."

At least one thing had changed for the better in Ruleville.

When Eddie left, most black people took care of their health problems with home remedies, or, at best, with the help of women who might have had some nursing experience. Otherwise, they had to go 14 miles into Cleveland, MS, to find the closest black doctor. Certainly no white doctor would touch them.

"Naw, I don't think I need a doctor, Pearline. This looks pretty good," he said, admiring her neat handiwork. "Thanks."

Eddie was thankful for more than Pearline's TLC. Dying is one thing, but damaging his arm and not being able to play anymore would have been much worse. He didn't know what Sonny had told her, but gratefully she didn't pepper him with questions.

"You're the best," he said, kissing her lightly on the cheek.

"Ya got that right. You hear that?" she said to Sonny, who was anxiously hovering in the hallway outside the bathroom.

"Don't let it go to your head, Florence Nightingale."

"Let's go, Sonny. The man's gotta get some rest," Pearline said, heading toward their bedroom.

"Be right there." Sonny grabbed Eddie's non-bandaged arm and pulled Eddie aside. "I didn't tell Pearline you'd been shot at. She thinks you were drunk and cut your arm against a piece of junk at the shop. It just reinforces her belief that drink can only lead to grief. But you better tell me what this is all about."

"Sonny, I wish I knew," Eddie said wearily.

"Does it have something to do with Sheriff Cooper's trial? It's not much of a secret you left right after Bertie's body was found. And I never believed that bullshit about you just happenin' to get a ride up North. But if I'd known it woulda put ya in danger, I'd have never asked ya to return."

"I told you, I don't know why I was shot at," Eddie repeated. "Maybe it would have just been better for everyone to let sleeping dogs lie."

"Well, the dogs are awake now. And it looks like you have a mighty angry hellhound on your trail."

## CHAPTER 17

*After a restless night* filled more with tossing and turning than sleep, Eddie finally gave up and rolled out of bed at 6:30. He didn't shower or shave and was out the door by 6:45, managing to avoid both Sonny and Pearline. He knew he was going to have to face a grilling from the sheriff as it was; he didn't want a warm-up, even from concerned friends.

As he drove to his meeting with the sheriff, a question with a seemingly unknowable answer played over and over in his mind like the proverbial broken record: Why had someone tried to kill him? His best guess was that it was a white supremacist who just didn't like any "uppity niggas" coming back who might stir things up. If Sonny had worked out that he was somehow connected to Bertie's death 30 years ago, even those dumb-as-dirt Klansmen could figure out the same thing.

His prime candidate for a new local Klansmen leader was Matt Cooper, Earl's nephew. Just keep your temper in check, Eddie told himself, and maybe Matt Cooper will reveal his true nature during this sham of an investigation. Now that he had experienced a different life away from Mississippi, it was hard for him to slip back into the old role that he grew up with. Shit, if he was honest with himself, he *still* had to put on an act to shield himself from abusive white authority. It was a matter of life and death then, and it was a matter of life and death today. Look at the recent beating of Rodney King right there in LA. Maybe in this day and age black men weren't being hung from trees or barn rafters, but that didn't mean they weren't being violently attacked or killed in other ways.

When Eddie arrived at the gray, low-slung building that housed the Sunflower County Sheriff's Department, the deputy at the front desk seemed to know who he was before he got his name out. He was ushered right into Cooper's private office. The sheriff gestured for him to sit down on a hard wooden chair facing his desk.

"How's that arm doing?" the sheriff asked.

"It's fine." Eddie had been cradling his bandaged arm, but now he let it drop by his side.

"I see you didn't heed my warning about staying out of trouble."

"You seem to forget *I'm* the one who was shot at," Eddie couldn't help but blurt out.

"Yes, you were shot at. And if the shooter had any better aim, you wouldn't be sitting here today having this conversation with me, so it would be in your best interest to answer my questions as truthfully and completely as possible. Let's start with this: Who would want you dead?"

"I ain't got the slightest idea."

"Maybe you've been messing around with someone's wife," the sheriff prompted.

"Isn't it *your* job to find out who shot at me?" Eddie said angrily.

"Mr. Baker, I'm trying to do my job. Your job here is to give me your full cooperation," the sheriff replied evenly. "Let's try this again. Who knew you were going to be playing at the garage last night?"

"We didn't exactly post flyers, but it wasn't a big secret either. Anybody walkin' by coulda seen us."

The sheriff studied his notes for a minute.

"What about the shell casings? Shouldn't they give you a lead?" Eddie demanded.

"They were common caliber shells from a 12-gauge shotgun. They could have come from any shotgun belonging to a hunter, which is 90% of the citizens of this county."

"Someone like you maybe. Are you talking about hunting turkeys . . . or maybe hunting something bigger?" Eddie replied, eyeing a prominent photograph of the previous sheriff, Earl Cooper, proudly holding a rifle.

Matt followed his eyes. "I won't say I don't love my uncle. I love the man because he's blood, but I hate everything he stood for," he said passionately. "I became a sheriff not because I wanted to carry on his legacy. I became a sheriff because I wanted to finally provide a level playing field for everyone, black and white. Now if you're honest with me, I promise I'll be honest with you."

Eddie still could find no reason to trust Matt Cooper, even if he wasn't a foaming-at-the-mouth racist. From the time Eddie was born until he left town, every white person in Ruleville had tried to take advantage of every black person they encountered.

"I've told you everything I know."

"Did you know your friend Skeeter was seen poking around the bushes at the crime scene early this morning?"

Eddie tried to hide his surprise. He just grunted noncommittedly.

"He took off before an officer could talk to him. Maybe he was looking for the shotgun he hid there. You know he's the only one at the garage last night who doesn't have someone to corroborate his whereabouts at the time of the shooting."

"What, one of my oldest friends has just been waiting all these years to take a shot at me?" Eddie snorted.

"I've seen stranger things. Jealousy can be a powerful emotion. The word is that some folks have nursed a bit of a grudge over you leaving Ruleville and having some success as a professional musician."

"Yeah, well they wouldn't be so jealous if they saw my bank account."

"All I'm saying is, watch your back. Here's my card in case you think of anything else. We'll be in touch as soon as I have any more information for you."

Raelene received a call from her Council buddy as soon as Eddie left the sheriff's office.

"You said to call you if Eddie Baker ever showed up here. Well, he just left. I can't tell ya what he was here for, though. The sheriff spoke to him alone in his office."

"Thanks, sugar. You did the right thing."

On the ride back to Sonny's house, Eddie entertained the possibility that maybe someone other than a rabid white supremacist would want him dead. He certainly didn't buy the sheriff's hint that Skeeter or anyone else was that jealous of him. It wasn't like he had ridden back into town in a brand-new Caddy, flashing a handful of diamond rings.

If Sonny was any indication, a lot of people seemed to think Eddie knew something about Bertie's killing he wasn't sharing. Maybe the sheriff was trying to throw Eddie off the trail of his own guilt. He had the biggest motive for trying to protect his uncle, no matter what he told Eddie. And Matt Cooper had shown up mighty fast after the shooting.

A crazy thought briefly surfaced. Maybe the intended target was Nick, not Eddie. They had been standing next to each other. No one would confuse a mid-sized black guy with that white Goliath, but they had been unsteadily weaving back and forth as they stood to take a leak. That could have thrown the shooter off. Nick hadn't been here long enough to make any enemies, but what about that LA cop that caught Nick with his wife? He could have found out that Nick had gone to Mississippi. It might be easier for him to eliminate Nick down here where no one could possibly connect him to the crime.

The only thing Eddie had to show from trying to figure it all out was a pounding headache. And that was on top of his throbbing arm. He'd kill right now for a good stiff drink, but he'd have to settle for some of Pearline's strong coffee. At least that would help clear his foggy mind. Then he'd have to find a way to contact Nick to let him know he was okay.

"Well, speak of the Devil," Eddie shouted when he entered Sonny's kitchen through the back door. Nick was wolfing down a hearty breakfast of bacon and eggs at the kitchen table. Eddie wasn't surprised to see him. He should have warned Pearline that feeding Nick once was like feeding a feral cat. It would keep showing up.

"Please, no idle talk about the Devil in this house," Pearline said indignantly.

"Sorry, Pearline."

"Are ya here to see me or just eat?" he asked Nick.

"No reason why I can't do both. Pearline assured me that it was a minor wound. You're lucky that shot . . ."

Eddie frantically waved his hand behind Pearline's back.

". . . of whiskey kept you from feeling the pain," Nick finished feebly.

Luther and Skeeter showed up a few minutes later.

"So how's the patient this morning?" Luther asked. "We wanted to check in on ya and say good-bye before leaving town. I'm needed back at the store."

"Yeah, ya gave us a bit of a scare last night," Skeeter admitted. "I didn't wanna go back to Louisiana worrying about ya."

"I'll live, thanks to having such good medical care," Eddie said, nodding at Pearline.

"Y'all want to sit down and have a cup of coffee?" she asked, removing Nick's vacuum-cleaned plate.

"Yes, ma'am!"

"Sounds good."

"Thanks."

"Why don't y'all go sit in the dining room and I'll bring some over."

"Sonny told her I cut my arm on a piece of junk. No need to worry her," Eddie whispered as soon as they sat down at the dining room table.

"No sense talking behind my back. I know a bullet wound when I see one," Pearline said when she returned with four steaming mugs of coffee. She placed them in front of her guests and took one for herself as she sat down next to Eddie.

"What did that cracker sheriff have to say?" Skeeter asked.

"He seems to think I brought this on myself. He had warned me before not to 'disturb the peace.' Shit! Maybe he thinks I enjoy being shot at."

"Yeah, it's peaceful unless you happen to be black," Luther said bitterly. "The Klan has crawled out from whatever rocks they've been hiding under and been in the spotlight since Earl Cooper was arrested. They've just been smart enough to trade their robes for suits, but they're the same snakes underneath. Did you see them on TV marching around the courthouse carrying signs? I heard one of them give an interview demanding that all charges be dropped because Earl Cooper was the *real* victim."

"Maybe someone in that group thinks you're one of those 'outside agitators' they're always carrying on about," Skeeter added.

"I might just be one if my music gets people to stand up for themselves."

"Well, if that's the case, we'd better be prepared for them to shoot at a helluva lot more black folks," Luther said to nods all around the table.

"Skeeter, the sheriff told me you were poking around in the bushes this morning. Lose something?" Eddie asked casually.

"As a matter of fact, I did," Skeeter replied, holding up a key-ring. "It musta fallen out of my pocket in all the excitement. I didn't notice it until I reached for my keys this morning."

"Little brother, you'd lose your head if it wasn't attached."

"Did you consider that whoever shot at ya last night might try again?" Pearline asked worriedly.

"Which is why right now is a good time to leave. Why don't you come back up to LA with me?" Nick urged. "I've got that extra helmet, and your skinny ass doesn't take up much room."

"I'm not running away . . . again."

The table was silent.

"Can we at least get out of town for a while? Maybe that'll give the shooter some time to cool off," Nick urged. "There's gotta be someplace outside of Ruleville you'd like to visit."

"Well, I wouldn't mind taking a ride out to Memphis," Eddie conceded. "I heard there's some hot new clubs that have opened on Beale Street. We could check them out."

"That's not a half-bad idea," Luther said. "If I can get someone to cover for me, I can beg off work for another day. What about you, little brother?"

"I'm not due back at the rig quite yet. And stop calling me *little brother.*"

"Pearline, is it okay if we steal your husband for a bit?" Eddie asked.

"It's up to him. It might be nice to get him out from under my feet for a bit at that."

When Eddie called up Sonny at the garage, he picked up on the first ring.

"I was just about to call you. Did ya hear the news? Someone just killed Rusty Miller while he was under police protection. It don't sound like they caught the shooter."

"Naw, I hadn't heard that."

"It seems like a mighty strange coincidence after last night. Is there something you haven't told me about your connection to Bertie's murder? Maybe that's why someone took a shot at you."

"Sonny, I have no idea what's going on and neither does the sheriff. I just got back from talking to him. I was calling to invite ya on a road trip to check out the blues scene on Beale Street. After everything that's happened, I could use a little vacation from my vacation. We're all going, me and Luther and Skeeter and Nick."

"Sound like a great idea, but I can't join you. I'm up to my neck in repairs. But look, I can lend you a van to use so you can travel together. It's fixed, but the owner can't pick it up for a couple of days. Just make sure you get it back in one piece."

"I promise."

"And Eddie, make sure you make it back in one piece too."

"Yeah, yeah. I already got Pearline worrying about me. I don't need you fussing over me too. Catch ya later."

As he hung up, Eddie guiltily remembered that he was supposed to talk to EJ today. If there was some madman out to get him, it would be better to see EJ sooner than later because there might not be a later. He didn't want to let his friends know how worried he was about his future. He faced them with a confident smile.

"Sonny can't make it, but it looks like we're going on a road trip courtesy of his loaner van. First, I have some business to take care of. Why don't we all meet up at the garage somewhere around 6:00 or so."

"Before you go anywhere, I need to take a look at your arm again," Pearline said firmly.

Pearline removed the dressing and examined the wound with a critical eye. "OK, I guess you can travel," she said as she put on a clean dressing. "Remember, if you run into any trouble in Memphis, Jesus is always right by your side."

"Yes, ma'am," Eddie said meekly.

Eddie smiled inwardly. He couldn't tell Pauline that he didn't want Jesus to help with the "trouble" he was looking forward to—red-hot blues, a gut full of cold beer, and maybe even some loose women if they were lucky.

## CHAPTER 18

*Eddie drove up* to the small cottage EJ shared with his fian-cée. The lawn was overdue for a mowing and filled with dande-lions. Obviously lawn care was not one of EJ's pastimes. There was a car parked in the driveway, so somebody was home. Eddie stood on the steps and knocked with more confidence than he felt. His heart skipped a beat when his son opened the screen door. EJ had his mother's large eyes and cherub-shaped mouth. He was the color of café au lait, lighter than either Rosalynn or himself. Eddie searched EJ's face for any sign that this was his son. A concrete, physical connection would go a long way in making his fatherhood seem real. Deep down, he was afraid that Rosalynn had made up the whole story about Eddie being EJ's father just to punish him.

"Yeah, whatcha want?" EJ asked.

"I'm Eddie Baker. I think your mother told ya I'd be stopping by. Can I come inside to talk? Please."

"Suit yourself. Just don't let the cat out."

EJ settled down on a couch covered with a colorful Indian bed-spread. He gestured for Eddie to sit down on a faded chintz arm-chair facing him across an old trunk serving as a coffee table. A scrawny tiger-striped cat gave Eddie the once-over and then disappeared under the couch.

"Sandra's out visiting her sister, so make this quick. I don't want ya here when she gets back."

"EJ, I won't beat around the bush. You know I'm your father; right?"

"That's what Mom says. So what? You never did a thing for me, or her. At least Uncle Earl, that ignorant cracker, gave us money. That money helped keep a roof over our heads and food on our table."

"Who's Uncle Earl?"

"Earl Cooper, the former sheriff."

"Why would *he* help you out?" Eddie asked, totally confused.

"I dunno. Maybe we were a convenient black charity after he found Jesus. Him and Mom prayed together and shit. All I know is he always gave me presents on my birthday and Christmas. Where were you all those times? Guess you were too busy being some kind of big-time musician to worry about us."

"Ya gotta believe me," Eddie said fervently. "I didn't know you even *existed* until I got back to Ruleville."

"Yeah, whatever." EJ said, shaking his head in disgust.

Eddie couldn't take his eyes off EJ's long fingers. They were only too familiar.

"And why you keep staring at my hands?"

"Sorry," Eddie said, self-consciously hiding his own long fingers by sitting on his hands. He looked around the room. Sitting in the corner was a guitar case. "You play?"

A small smile finally curled around the ends of EJ's mouth. "I play, but I don't play any of that old-timey shit you blues guys play."

"So what kind of music do you like?"

"I like to listen to N.W.A., Sir-Mix-a Lot, and Ice Cube. For axe playing, though, Hendrix was the shit." EJ's eyes lit up. "The man knew how to rock. Nobody else can play like Hendrix."

"Ya know Hendrix was firmly rooted in the blues and really looked up to Muddy Waters and Albert King."

"Who?"

Eddie opened his mouth in astonishment and then shut it.

"Listen, I know I can never make up for all the time I wasn't here. But I would like to get to know you better. Maybe you'll decide to get to know me. Lord knows I've made my share of mistakes, but I'm really trying to do better. Here's my phone number in LA," Eddie scrawled it on the inside of a matchbook cover. "Call me anytime."

EJ folded his arms over his chest. Eddie left the matchbook on top of the coffee table.

"At least go listen to Muddy and Albert," Eddie said on the way out the door. It was the best advice he could pass on to his son.

A tsunami of sadness washed over him when he drove off. Bertie's murder not only had robbed Eddie and Rosalynn of normal lives, but it had robbed EJ of so much too. EJ made a big show of being totally indifferent toward him, maybe too big of a show. Eddie was sure it was masking a deep well of hurt and resentment. Eddie never forgave his own father for walking out on his family. A strange thought popped into his head. There were times growing up when Eddie fantasized about exacting revenge on his absent father. Could his own son hate him enough to try to shoot him?

CHAPTER 19

//////////////////////////////////////////////////////////////////////////////

**Beale Street.** The name struck a chord in the heart of every true blues lover. Its role as a center of black life and music had been a wild rollercoaster ride. W.C. Handy, considered by many the "father of the blues," had written the first published blues song, *Memphis Blues*, there in September 1912. The street throbbed with music venues and black-owned businesses in the 1920s. Even during the Depression, Beale Street was a vibrant mix of clubs, businesses, and shops frequented by politicians and less-legitimate hustlers, ministers of music and ministers of the cloth. Riley B. King moved to Memphis in 1946. He was originally dubbed Beale Street Blues Boy. Blues Boy was shortened to B.B. and the rest is history.

Bobby "Blue" Bland arrived in Memphis in 1947. He brought his soulful voice to amateur shows at the Palace Theater. There were lots of young blues musicians to mix with on Beale Street. The blues gods helped B.B. and Bobby find each other. The guitarist/radio DJ and singer struck up what was to be a lifelong friendship.

But in the 1960s, the street started falling on hard times. As the beginning of integration opened more opportunities for black people, they started businesses in other areas. The clubs closed and people moved on. In the name of "urban renewal," many historic buildings were torn down, including the Palace Theater in the 1970s. The street was eventually condemned.

But now it was back up on the top of the rollercoaster loop. In the 1980s, the street made a comeback. Elkington & Keltner, a private non-profit corporation, was chosen by the City of Memphis to turn the street around. It focused on making Beale "Home of the Blues" once more. With music clubs, bars, and restaurants jammed into a three-block historic area, it was a draw for thousands of music pilgrims from all over the country. Eddie and his friends couldn't resist its siren call either.

It was like herding cats, but by 6:30 that evening, Skeeter, Eddie, and Nick were loaded in the van with Luther at the wheel. They didn't expect to be back in Ruleville until the wee hours of the next day. Nick was "volunteered" to be their "designated driver" on the way home.

"I don't mind," Nick said, "but wouldn't one of you guys know these roads better than me?"

"Shit, Nick. Let me explain the facts of life," Skeeter said disgustedly. "A white driver has less of a chance of being pulled over. We've seen what happens when a state trooper pulls over a bunch of brothers with no one else around. It ain't pretty, which is why we need your ugly white face in the driver's side window. Got it?"

Eddie tensed up. The van got ominously quiet.

"Ugly? Who you callin' ugly, man? Look at you. Eddie told me when you were born, the doctor slapped you on your butt, put you down, and then the nurse got one in too!"

Eddie and Luther burst into laughter. Even Skeeter couldn't help but join in.

"Everybody comfortable and don't need to see a man about a horse?" Luther asked. "I don't wanna have to stop before Memphis."

Eddie sang the first couple of lines of Muddy Waters' *I'm Ready*, which everybody joined in on.

"Home of the blues, here we come!" Nick said excitedly.

"Ya know, I always wanted to go on tour with a blues band," Skeeter said.

"What, you think we travel around with a liveried chauffeur while sipping champagne in the back seat of a limo and every night we have to beat the groupies off with sticks?" Eddie snorted. "Let me tell ya'll what touring's *really* like."

"You got four or five cats in a van with the equipment in a trailer behind. We're like truck drivers, except for one main difference. After we haul the shit and unload the shit, we don't go to a hotel or back of the cab to sleep; we play to 2:00 in the morning. Then we meet the fans, hang out, pack up the shit, and hit the road to the next place. If we're lucky, that's just 300 miles down the road. Then we check into the hotel for a few hours' rest and head on to the gig. Maybe we can eat at the gig, maybe not. So we do a lot of 'Cuisine Waffle House' and Popeyes. Sometimes we get lucky and can stay at a hotel after the gig if the next day's drive ain't too bad. And most of the damn hotels we get ain't even Motel 6, they more like Motel 3. Shit, when I start making it big, I'm gonna put in the contract rider: NO HOTEL WITH A NUMBER IN ITS NAME!"

"Man, you got that right," Nick said. "That's why I got my camping gear. Sleeping on the ground is better than some of the shithole hotels I've been in. And I ain't even a struggling musician."

"And don't get me started about the money! The man says he gonna pay you this, and then the end of the night he say something like: 'You all sounded real good, but we didn't do what I thought we would. We a little light tonight.'"

"Our bandleader tells him, 'Man, the house was damn near full on a Thursday night!'"

"Then the man tells him, 'Yeah, but they wasn't drinking.'"

"What are we gonna do? Draw a gun on the motherfucker? He probably got his protection ready before he says that shit to you. So you get your little money and pack the shit up and head on out hoping the next night will be better or at least somewhat right."

"You know, I almost feel sorry for the bandleader. He gotta pay the band what he told them they was getting. If he don't do that, he ain't gonna have a band. Then what's he gonna do? So who ends up being really light? And I ain't even talking about covering the hotels on the nights off and some kinda money for food. Don't even think about getting me started with the band complaining or the girlfriends and the wives complaining! Shit, you ever hear that William Clarke song *The Complainer's Boogie Woogie?*"

"Damn, I sure didn't know it was like that!" Skeeter said, shaking his head. "Man, it's always good to get the story from the part of the horse that goes over the fence first."

"Mmm-hmm. Well, now, if I had a hit record that might change things a bit."

"Bet that would change a whole lotta things," Luther added.

"You got that right," Eddie replied. "I'll have to get Pearline praying on it."

That set the whole gang laughing.

They made it to Beale Street in good time, despite Luther being careful never to go over the speed limit and attract the attention of any highway patrols. Luther found a parking spot off of Union Avenue. When they hit Beale Street, they saw a small group of tourists gathered around a tuxedo-clad street performer blowing a mean trumpet. It was none other than Rudy Williams, a decades-long blues fixture known as "The Mayor of Beale Street." They listened to him play *The St. Louis Blues* and dropped some bills in his bucket. He tipped his bowler hat and went right on playing.

Nick stood spellbound in the middle of the street, torn between the recently opened B. B. King's Blues Club and the Rum Boogie

Cafe. As usual, his stomach had the deciding vote. Rum Boogie advertised "Down Home Cookin', Down Home Blues."

"Look," Nick rapturously exclaimed, "they serve fried catfish, country-fried steak, pulled pork sandwiches . . . I might have to get one of each."

"Yeah, but more importantly, I see Son Seals is on the menu tonight," Eddie said. "Ya'll are in for a real tasty evening. Wait here a minute. I want to check something out."

Eddie went around back to where a van was disgorging band members and instruments. Son was nowhere to be found, but Eddie recognized the drummer from his days in Chicago.

"Hey there, Tony. How's it goin', man?"

"Sweet Eddie! It's been a while. You livin' in Memphis now, or are you just giggin' at another club?"

"Just down here visiting with some friends. Any chance you can get us some good seats for the show?"

"No problem. But listen, Eddie," Tony said, looking around, "I hope you weren't thinking of asking to sit in. The big guy ain't into that."

"Man, I totally understand. It's only good when you know the cat and have played with him. Some guys you invite to sit in think it's their show then and just fuck it up."

"I know you right. I remember one night in Chicago this harp player wanted to sit in. Son musta been in a generous mood, because he said 'OK.' Man, that fool just played over every damn thing. Son was singing; he was playing. The piano player took a solo; he was playing. It was pitiful. He never stopped playing. The only space he used was the one he was taking up."

Eddie laughed. "Yeah, I can dig it."

"Now I can play a little harp and I know when a cat only knows the second position, from the 1st hole to the 6th hole. If the crowd is drunk enough, they think it's great. Then the fool gets inspired to do more. Now the great harp players—like George Harmonica Smith, The Walters, Musselwhite, and them—can play in 1st, 2nd, 3rd, and hell, I don't know, maybe even 4th and 5th!" Tony said with a big smile. "That's serious harp playing."

"You got that right, Tony. Hey, now I won't be sittin' in, but I can't say I won't be trying to steal some of Son's stuff!" Eddie said, laughing.

Tony chuckled. "I hear you, brother. Okay then. I got you covered. Meet me at this door in about 30 minutes."

Eddie rejoined his friends. "We're in luck. I ran into some cat I know and he's getting us primo seats."

"Sounds good to me," Skeeter said.

"You know that's right," Luther added.

"Let's go over to A. Schwab's variety store for a little bit. I've heard they have everything you want and lots you don't even know you want. I want to bring back a box of candy for Pearline."

After browsing around the merchandise-jammed store for a while and debating which candy to buy, they made it back in time to get seated at a table close to the stage and order some beer and food before Son's band started. True to form, Nick ordered fried catfish, country-fried steak, *and* a pulled pork sandwich!

"Are ya ordering for the table, or is this all for you?" the waitress asked, looking up from her order pad.

"Oh, this is my dinner. I have no idea what these guys want."

Luther shook his head. "Just make sure there's room on the table for the rest of our dinners."

"Ya'll be filling up on the real good stuff once Son plays," Eddie promised his friends.

"I've heard of him," Luther said. "His father owned some kinda club in Osceola, Arkansas, where one of my friends used to hang out. He said that even as a teenager, Son was something special."

"Albert King played in that club too. He musta rubbed off on Son. Albert and him are both intense players that got fierce personalities. I'm not surprised one of Son's albums was called *Live and Burning*. I must have played that album to death, and it was almost the death of me," Eddie said with a laugh.

How could Eddie describe Son's live performance? Soulful. Scorching. Unrelenting. Urgent. Son Seals' ferocious singing and axe wielding were all that and more. When he launched into *Funky Bitch*, the Mississippi friends watched his fingers yank the notes from his guitar—and seemingly right from their guts.

After a couple more songs that left Son glistening with sweat, Eddie and company needed to cool off also. They eagerly gulped down the rest of the pitcher of beer they had started with dinner and signaled the waitress for another one. This performance was a workout for the band *and* the audience.

Eddie went over to thank the drummer during the break between sets. Luther and Skeeter drifted over to talk to other members of the band to tell them how much they enjoyed their playing. Nick stayed seated with his eyes closed. He had reached a state of total bliss, both from the music and the food.

"Tony, I don't even know what to say. Is he always like that?" Eddie nodded at Son, who was at the end of the bar by himself, hunched over a drink. The joy that Son radiated from playing seemed to have evaporated.

"Every song. Every night," the drummer answered, shaking his head.

Eddie walked toward the end of the bar to pay his respects. Son lifted his head and fixed him with a look that had *fuck off* written all over it. Eddie took the hint and rejoined his friends.

By the time the second set was over, they left feeling like they had survived a Category 5 hurricane. They were wrung-out, sopping wet, and almost too tired for words. But man, it was totally worth it.

Skeeter sat up front with Nick for the trip home. They were having a good-natured argument about whose version of *Crawlin'*

*King Snake* was better, Big Joe Williams' or John Lee Hooker's. Listening to their back and forth, Eddie realized Skeeter wasn't seeing black or white, just another cat into the blues.

Yeah, the blues will do that, Eddie happily thought. He leaned back and closed his eyes. As he was about to doze off, a loud bang jolted him fully awake. The van swerved into the next lane. He looked around wildly. Was someone shooting at him again?

"What the hell was that?" Luther exclaimed.

"Shit. The car in front of us hit a deer. The deer ran off though. I hope it'll be okay," Nick said wistfully. "Maybe we should turn around and look for it to make sure."

"No! Hell no! Don't even think about it," was the resounding chorus from his passengers.

Eddie was too wound up to go back to sleep. When he closed his eyes, images of a deer, bleeding to death in the woods, metamorphosed into an image of himself lying bleeding on the ground, with a triumphant hunter standing over him. He couldn't see the face of the hunter, but Eddie knew he was still out there, waiting for him.

CHAPTER 20

**After Nick** dropped off Skeeter and Luther, Eddie took over and dropped Nick off at his campsite. Eddie parked the van in the driveway in front of Sonny's garage and promptly fell asleep. He was having a pleasant dream about headlining at the Rum Boogie when Sonny knocked on the van's front door.

"Wake up now," Sonny yelled.

Eddie stretched his stiff back. "OK, OK. I'm awake. No need to holler."

Sonny gave the van a once-over.

"Is that big smile for seeing me or the van back in one piece?" Eddie asked, pressing the van keys into Sonny's hand.

"Both."

"Ya sure did miss some kind of trip. We saw Son Seals at the Rum Boogie Cafe. Man, that cat's for real! And we didn't even have a chance to check out the new B.B. King's Club."

"I'll make it to Beale Street one of these days," Sonny said longingly.

"Did I miss anything while we were gone?"

"As a matter of fact, we had some, let's say, excitement while you were gone. I think you better see for yourself."

There was no missing the "excitement" when they pulled up in front of Sonny's house. One of the big windows in the front had been smashed.

"What the fuck, Sonny! Are you and Pearline all right?"

"Pearline was shaken up, as you can imagine, but we're both okay."

"What happened?"

"I heard breaking glass early this morning. When I came downstairs, I found a brick with a note had been tossed through the window."

"What did the note say?"

"'Death to all uppity niggers and their nigger friends.' It was signed 'KKK' in blood. I guess they think black folks faint at the sight of blood. There was a noose hanging from the porch light. The sheriff took everything away to examine."

When they went inside, Pearline was doggedly sweeping up the broken glass. There were still scattered shards that crunched underfoot. She dropped the broom when they walked in.

"Oh, Eddie. You're okay! I was so worried about ya."

"I'm so sorry, Pearline. I didn't mean to bring any trouble to your home."

"It's not your fault, young man."

A man Eddie hadn't noticed when he entered the house rose from a chair.

"Eddie, this is Reverend Isaiah Harris. He's the pastor at our church."

"Reverend Harris, this is the friend I told ya about, Eddie Baker."

Eddie shook hands with the dignified older man. There was more strength in his handshake than his silver hair would have indicated.

Pearline noticed the look of surprise on Eddie's face. "The reverend tries to keep our teenagers out of trouble by teaching them boxing."

"Eddie, Pearline and I already talked to Sheriff Cooper. I promised you'd go talk to him as soon as you got back."

"Why ain't the sheriff and his officers here to protect ya'll?"

"This house *is* under protection," Reverend Harris rumbled. "Our congregation has agreed to take turns watching the house, day and night. We believe in peace, but we also believe in defending ourselves." He nodded toward the baseball bat that was resting against the chair. "And of course we have the best protection of all. We're under the wings of the Heavenly Father."

A well-cushioned woman straining the seams of a snug cream-colored dress came out of the kitchen wielding a huge kitchen knife. A smaller, younger woman timidly trailed in her wake.

"Sister Pearline, can I use this to cut my icebox cake?"

"Mmm-hmm. That's fine."

The woman noticed Eddie and stopped in her tracks.

"This here's our friend, Eddie Baker."

"Eddie, this is Sister Gloria Bailey and her daughter Della."

"I remember Gloria. Nice to meet ya, Della."

"Uh-huh. I remember Eddie." She looked him up and down. He got the distinct impression he was found wanting. Della smiled shyly at him.

"Sister Pearline, you weren't with us when his mother and aunt were in the church choir. They were something special. We never got to hear Eddie sing, though. I heard he chose to use his God-given talents *outside* the church."

"Eddie, why don't ya sit down in the dining room," Pearline broke into the awkward silence. "As soon as I finish cleaning up this mess, we'll be ready for our prayer meeting. If you don't want to pray, you can still join us in some after-meeting refreshments. Ya don't want to miss Sister Gloria's justifiably famous cake."

"When Sister Pearline called to tell us she couldn't make our prayer meeting this morning and why, we decided to bring the prayer meeting to her," Gloria said, smiling fondly at Pearline.

"Thanks, Pearline, but I think I better go see the sheriff right away. If ya'll excuse me, I'll give him a call and let him know I'm on the way over."

As Eddie went up the steps, he couldn't miss Gloria's loud aside.

"I heard he's *still* playing the Devil's music, and I could smell the liquor on him. If any man needs to pray for forgiveness, it's Eddie Baker."

Eddie couldn't hear Pearline's muffled reply. Maybe that was for the best. After grabbing a quick shower and changing his clothes, he felt ready to face the sheriff.

Sonny had grabbed some plastic sheets and duct tape out of the garage. He was taping the broken window when Eddie was getting ready to leave.

"Sonny, are you sure you're safe?"

"Truth is, the more we cower like some whipped dogs and don't stand up for ourselves, the less safe we are. The days of being scared off by a bunch of motherfuckin' crackers are over! Besides, I have more faith in those determined church members than the whole white sheriff's department. Would you want to mess with the good reverend or Sister Gloria?"

"Suppose not."

"We'll be fine. It's you I'm worried about."

When Eddie entered the sheriff's office, two men in dark suits and white shirts were stiffly standing behind the sheriff.

"I can't tell ya'll nothing about that note," Eddie said quickly.

"Mr. Baker, these gentlemen are here to ask you a few questions about your shooting incident. They believe your shooting is connected to the Rusty Miller killing. The incident at the Jacksons' has all the hallmarks of a federal hate crime. The FBI has also teamed up with us local guys and is providing its special resources to investigate it. No matter what you may think, we're all here to help you. The only way we can do that is for you to help us. I hope you'll cooperate."

The slightly older-looking one, a grave man with a military-style crewcut, spoke first.

"Mr. Baker, I'm William Dickinson from the District Attorney's office. This here's Assistant DA Montgomery Webster," he said, pointing to his equally somber colleague, a younger version of himself with slightly longer hair. "Please sit down."

"I'm going to be frank with you, Mr. Baker," Dickinson continued. "Now that Rusty Miller is out of the picture, it looks like all charges will be dropped against Mr. Cooper. I'm sure none of us want that. The Sunflower County DA's office has worked extremely hard to prove that it can handle this kind of racially charged case without relying on the Feds. We're committed to following every lead to get a conviction."

"And you think someone taking a shot at me is some kind of lead?"

"It looks to us like someone out there, someone who will stop at nothing to destroy our case, thinks you're a lead. We've been told that you left town the day Bertie's body was found. If you have any information about what happened to him, now is the time to come forward. We can assure you that anything you tell us will be kept confidential."

"What, are you going to protect me like you protected Rusty?"

"Mr. Baker, there are no guarantees in life, but you have my word we'll do our best. I can tell you that your perceived connection to this case has now put your friends' lives in danger. Don't *they* at least deserve your help?"

Eddie stared at the white men one by one. Were any of them worthy of his trust? Eddie was still suspicious of where Matt Cooper's loyalties really lay. In the South, blood came first. Maybe the sheriff's little speech was all for show.

As if reading his mind, the sheriff shifted uneasily in his seat.

"I'll talk to you two, but not in front of him," he said, jerking him thumb at the sheriff.

DA Dickinson did not hesitate. "Sheriff Cooper, do you have an interrogation room we can use, privately?"

The two attorneys and Eddie sat down on metal chairs at a table ringed with old coffee stains. The airless room reeked of a pungent blend of cigarette smoke and stale sweat. Eddie tried not to think about all the black men who had been threatened, and worse, during interrogations in this very room in the not-so-distant past.

Dickinson turned on a tape recorder and explained that they would be recording the interview. Webster placed a small notebook and pen on the table.

I'm a dead man anyway, Eddie thought. There are no secrets in Ruleville. The word will get out that I've been talking to the DA's office. I might as well go down swinging.

"Now, what do you want to tell us?"

The words rushed out in a torrent—about the storm, about the barn, about the five white men, and finally, with his voice cracking, the awful details of the lynching.

Webster silently took notes. When Eddie finally stopped talking, Dickinson started asking him questions. If they were surprised by anything he told them, their blank expressions didn't give them away.

"We're going to investigate everything you said further. If it all checks out, would you be willing to testify in court about this?"

He heard someone saying "Yes, I'm willing to testify." Someone else had taken over Eddie's voice, a brave person inside of Eddie whom Eddie didn't know existed. It seemed that person was in the driver's seat, so all Eddie could do was go along for the ride.

"Sit tight, Mr. Baker. We'll be right back."

"Do you want a Coke or something?" Webster asked.

"A Coke would be good . . . unless you can get me something a little stronger."

Webster cracked a smile. "Sorry, a Coke's the best I can do."

Sitting tight wasn't really an option. Once the DAs left the room, Eddie furiously smoked while pacing the room.

The two attorneys returned about 20 minutes later, although it felt like an eternity to Eddie. They again sat down across from him. Webster handed him a can of soda.

Eddie turned the can around and around in his hands. Its moist coolness felt good against his burning palms.

"We appreciate your cooperation." Dickinson looked Eddie squarely in the eye. "I have to tell you, though, that with Rusty Miller out of the picture, even *with* your testimony, it's going to be a difficult case to prove."

Webster studied the stains on the table as if they were some secret code he was trying to decipher.

"Earl Cooper made a lot of self-incriminating statements at the time of the crime. Hell, he even bragged about the lynching. But most of the people he spoke to are dead or won't testify. There's no forensic evidence tying Earl Cooper to the murder. Would you be willing to try something risky, even riskier than testifying, to help us?"

*Would you be willing to die to get Bertie justice?* is the question you should be asking me, he thought. But Eddie knew the answer to that. He was more afraid of letting Bertie down again than losing his own life. Eddie nodded his assent.

Dickinson outlined his proposed plan. "Afterwards, you'll go right into protective custody."

"I have to make some phone calls first. And I need to get my guitar and bag from my friend's house."

"We'll send someone over to get your things, and we'll keep an eye on the Jacksons. You can make some calls, but you can't tell *anyone* what's going on. No one, and we mean no one," Dickinson said, looking meaningfully in the direction of the sheriff's private office, "outside of this room can learn what we're planning."

Eddie spoke to Sonny first.

"Listen, something urgent has come up and I gotta disappear for a while. I can't tell ya any more than that. I hope I've made the right decision, for all of us. Someone from the DA's office will pick up my bag and guitar. They'll be watching your house. A little extra protection besides the 'church brigade' can't hurt. Please put Pearline on the line."

"Pearline, I can't thank ya enough for all the kindness you've shown me, but I gotta leave. I'm trying to do what's best to help all of us. In my book, you're a true saint, especially for putting up with Sonny all these years."

Pearline laughed. "I hope we'll be seeing you again, real soon. I'll be praying for ya, baby. We all will be praying for ya."

"And I'll need every one of those prayers. Let me speak to Sonny again."

"I know Nick will be showing up on your doorstep. Tell him I got a call for a great gig and I gotta take it. I'll be back in LA as soon as I can. Tell him also that I'm counting on him to hurry on home to watch over Sylvia. If he asks about your window, tell him some kid threw a baseball through it. If you tell him the truth, he'll move in with ya. If he gives you a hard time, you can honestly say you have no idea where I went. Remember, I love ya, man."

Sonny didn't hesitate. "I love ya too, brother. Take care now."

Eddie made his last phone call to Sylvia.

"Sylvia, I'll be out of touch for a while. I'll explain everything when I get home."

"Eddie, are you OK? You don't sound like yourself."

"That's because this here's finally the real me. No more hiding behind booze or lies. I've learned something important. You can't be honest with others until you're honest with yourself. I realized I never told you how much I love you. I want us to get married as soon as I get home. What do ya say?"

"I'll think about it, Eddie."

That wasn't the answer Eddie had hoped for, but it was a start.

## CHAPTER 21

*Raelene was* speaking so excitedly on the line that Tucker could barely understand her.

"Slow down, honey, and start from the beginning."

"I'm so proud of you for taking care of Rusty Miller. I was afraid you didn't have it in ya," she gushed. "My contact in the sheriff's office told me that you almost took out that nigga boy too. It's a damn shame you missed. I didn't want you to have all the fun, so I sent a little message to that boy."

"What kind of message?"

"The kind of message that smashes through windows at night. If that doesn't do it, the next time it'll be a firebomb. I got everything ready for it."

"Raelene, that's great, but I gotta take care of something with my cousin. You got me just as I was walking out the door. I'll talk to you later."

Raelene was disappointed that Tucker didn't want to meet with her right that second to celebrate. She was so fired up she could hardly stand it. Well, it would give her time to pick up a bottle of champagne on the way home for a private party when they did get together. Their blows for white power deserved to be toasted with something more exciting than a couple of beers.

The DA's office held a press conference the next morning. "DA Dickinson is going to read a short statement," the office spokesman announced. "We're not taking any questions at this time."

"A new witness in the Earl Cooper case has come forward," Dickinson read from a sheet of paper. "He's promised to provide some physical evidence tying Earl Cooper to the scene of the crime."

"Who's this new witness?" a reporter demanded.

"What kind of evidence?" another reporter shouted out.

"That's all we have to say at this time."

Dickinson walked away without saying another word. He went back to his office, waited a few minutes, and then slipped out the back way. After making sure he wasn't being followed, the DA went to a drive-in restaurant out on Rte 8. Eddie was anxiously waiting for him in Webster's car, which was parked in the back of the lot.

Webster had tried to keep him busy talking about music, sports, anything but what was going to go down in a little while. Webster's musical taste seemed to be limited to Grand Ole Opry country, but Eddie made a game stab at broadening his horizons.

Dickinson slid into the back seat as Eddie was explaining that Hank Williams Sr. had learned the blues from Rufus Payne, aka Tee Tot, a black bluesman in Alabama, when Hank was just a young boy.

"The trap's been set. It's up to you now. Just follow the plan we discussed and you'll be alright," Dickinson said confidently. "Good luck."

"Well, this piece of bait needs all the luck he can get. I'll have a little more sympathy for worms next time I go fishing, *if* I ever go fishing again."

"Tell you what. If everything goes well, I'll take you fishing myself when the trial's over."

Someone drove up in a car. The driver got out and handed the keys to Eddie before climbing into Dickinson's car.

"Are you sure no one followed you here?" Dickinson asked.

"The coast is clear."

Eddie turned to Webster.

"Promise me you'll at least check out Clarence Gatemouth Brown. I think you'll like him."

"It's a deal, Eddie."

As Eddie drove to the Taylor farm early that evening, he glanced nervously at his back mirror. If someone was following him, they were doing a good job of staying out of sight. Dickinson was gambling that the killer had to be somebody who knew where the scene of the crime was and would be watching it to see if Eddie showed up there to uncover the mysterious "evidence." This wasn't gambling on a hand of blackjack where he had a slight edge on the odds. The DA was gambling with his life.

The farm looked peaceful in the soft twilight. Eddie slowly walked to the crumbling barn. Now I know what they mean by "dead man walking," Eddie thought to himself. The only sound was the sorrowful cry of a mourning dove. At least he hoped it was a mourning dove and not the cries of Bertie's restless spirit. He took a shovel out of the trunk and went to the spot behind the barn described by the DA. It had been painstakingly camouflaged with dead leaves. The spot was out of the line of sight from the house.

Eddie said a quick prayer and started digging. Without even thinking about it, he started humming a melody.

Where'd this song come from? Eddie wondered.

He dug a little more, still humming. Then it came to him. It was part of the old Leadbelly song *Poor Howard* that Otha absentmindedly sang when he was outside the house hanging his laundry on the line. Maybe it was a sign that Otha's spirit was there, keeping an eye on him from above. He sure hoped so.

Eddie quietly sang, his strokes keeping rhythm with the song.

> *Poor Howard, he dead and gone*
> *Mmm-hmm, dead and gone*
> *Left me here to carry on.*

He paused. His ears cocked for the slightest sound. Nothing. He resumed digging and singing.

> *Who been here since I been gone?*
> *Pretty little gal with a red dress on.*

His every nerve was strained, listening. Finally, he heard a faint crunch of wheels on the gravel. A car door opened and shut so softly that he felt it more than heard it. He willed himself to keep singing and digging and not turn around. Eddie broke out into a sweat as he piled up more and more dirt. His shovel hit something hard. He pulled out a small wooden box. Behind him, there was the unmistakable sound of a shotgun being cocked.

CHAPTER 22

Eddie turned around to see Rosalynn aiming a shotgun at him that seemed almost as big as she was. His shocked brain frantically tried to make some sense out of what he was seeing.

Rosalynn seemed to take some pleasure out of Eddie's stunned silence. "Yeah, that's right, I'm in control of your life now. How does it feel to have all your choices taken away from you?"

"I don't understand," Eddie stammered. "I thought I explained why I left. You know, you have to know, that I'd have been back sooner if I'd known about EJ. I know I fucked up, but this ain't gonna help anybody. Do you really hate me enough to kill me?"

"Hate you? Yes, I hate you. I hate Earl Cooper. I hate myself most of all. But you're the one who's forced me into this life and you're the one who's trying to take away what little life I have left," she said, tightening her grip on the gun.

"I still don't understand. What does Earl Cooper have to do with us?"

"Oh, he is part of 'us.' That night, that awful night, was the beginning of the end for all of us. I waited for you, waited for hours. I was desperate to talk to you, to tell you I was pregnant.

I was so relieved when I finally heard footsteps. I ran to the window and waved. But it wasn't you. It was Sheriff Cooper, drunk as a skunk, weaving along the riverfront. I ducked, but he'd already seen me in the window. You think I had a chance against him? And who was I going to tell about it afterwards? I vowed he was going to pay for what he did, one way or the other."

"When I had our son, who was kinda high yella, I decided to tell the sheriff it was his child. EJ's real name is EJ, not Eddie Junior. I told Cooper it was Earl Junior. Either he had to help us, or I'd tell everyone it was his son. And not only that, it was his child not conceived by rape, but because he had fallen in love with a colored girl. My momma used to clean for Miz Cooper, a sickly woman who never had kids. She used to complain about her life to my momma. Can you imagine? Some white lady who never worked a day in her life had the nerve to moan and groan about her life to my hardworking momma, who was bent over after years of scrubbing floors and lugging heavy loads of laundry. I threatened to tell Miz Cooper all about her husband's colored mistress and bastard child if he didn't help me. That would have about killed off that uppity racist bitch. So he paid, all these years he paid."

Eddie tried to stall for time. "Is that why you never got in touch with me?"

"What, some sneaking-off boy I knew I couldn't rely on? If it wasn't for Earl, I don't know how EJ and I would have survived. EJ was born with a hole in his heart and needed an operation plus special care and expensive medicine. I couldn't have put all that on my momma. She had lots of other grandbabies to worry about too. So I stayed home to take care of him and didn't work for the longest time. But thanks to Earl, EJ got his medicine and we always had food on the table."

"I'm sorry I wasn't there for you and our son. Let me make up for it. I don't make much, but I'll send as much as I can."

Rosalynn went on as if she hadn't heard him.

"But the surprising thing is that he loves that child. He so desperately wanted a son that he was able to look past his racism—somehow convince himself that this black child was different, worthy of being considered a real person. And after several years, he and I came to an understanding. When he secretly visited EJ, he also started secretly visiting me."

"I can't believe you let that monster put his hands on you, after what he did to you and knowing what he did to Bertie."

"I'd have let the Devil himself have me if it woulda helped my son. And now you've come back, stirring this all up. You want to get rid of Earl and take EJ away. I can't allow that," she said straightening up the shotgun that had begun to waver. "Now hand over that box!"

"What about Bertie? Doesn't he deserve justice?"

"Not only Bertie but there's a lot of other dead black people who are still crying out for justice," she said so softly that Eddie had trouble hearing her. "But Earl changed. I changed him. He has truly repented and made his peace with the Lord. What will be served by sending him to prison now? And if he's convicted, all his money will be seized to pay retribution. I need that money. I *earned* that money."

Eddie desperately tried to think of an answer. How could he convince Rosalynn that justice for Bertie's death was also justice for her, for all the other black women and children whose lives had been destroyed by racism? That killing him was another wrong that would never make what happened right.

"I'm done talking. Good-bye, Eddie," she said, aiming the gun at his head.

So this is how it ends, he thought. Not stabbed in a beer-soaked bar fight, not in a car crash on the way back from a gig, but in a peaceful setting with the rich aroma of blooming magnolias in the air.

"Drop the gun." Sheriff Matt Cooper's voice rang out from the woods directly behind Rosalynn. Rosalynn didn't flinch. She didn't turn around. She calmly took the shotgun, put it in her mouth, and pulled the trigger.

And just like that night so long ago, Eddie couldn't stop a terrible act from happening right before his eyes. And just as surely as he had once felt that noose closing around his neck, he felt himself exploding into a thousand pieces.

CHAPTER 23

**Raelene was** awakened by a loud pounding on her front door. She wrapped herself in a bathrobe and went downstairs. When she opened the door, Tucker stood on the doorstep along with two other men she had never seen. They were all wearing bullet-proof vests emblazoned with "FBI." The other men had their guns drawn and aimed at her.

"Tucker, I don't understand. What are you doing here? Who are these men?"

"It's actually Special Agent Jesse McKinley," he replied, showing her his FBI badge.

"Is this some kind of joke? If so, it ain't a bit funny, Tucker."

"It's Special Agent Jesse McKinley," he repeated. "And there's nothing funny about your recent activities. I was assigned to track down an out-of-state gunrunner we think is supplying weapons to certain members of the Council. I hated to break cover, but I couldn't wait any longer, not when lives were in imminent danger."

"I think I'm gonna faint," Raelene said, clutching the doorframe.

"Let's go in the living room and you can sit down." Jesse said, starting to enter.

"I don't want any damn race traitor setting foot in my house!" Raelene exclaimed, straightening up.

"Fine, then we'll do this on your doorstep. Raelene Taylor, you're under arrest for making terrorist threats pursuant to Federal hate crime statutes. Turn around, please." As he put handcuffs on her, he intoned the necessary Miranda warning, beginning with, "You have the right to remain silent and refuse to answer questions."

That wasn't enough to deter Raelene. She had too many questions of her own.

"But you killed Rusty Miller and tried to kill Eddie Baker," she blurted out.

"Sorry to disappoint you, but it wasn't me. There was actually someone else who wanted Earl Cooper protected. It's a long story, but you'll have plenty of time to read about it in prison."

"You got nothing on me. The lawyer I work for will have me out of jail so fast your head will spin. Besides, who's going to believe the word of an ex-con?"

"I have a recording of a certain conversation we had on the phone recently. It was enough to convince a judge to issue a search warrant. And the only time I've set foot in prison was to interview a criminal housed there."

"Search the house," he told the other agents. "Look for any traces of animal blood and materials to make a firebomb. And make sure you search behind the garbage can underneath the kitchen sink. She's got some guns hidden there."

"I still don't understand. I've heard you say you hate niggas over and over again. Why would you betray your own people?"

"I said and did anything and everything I could in order to keep an eye on the White Citizens Council," he said grimly. "It was my job. Besides, my black wife understands and totally supports me in that job."

"You mean you've kissed a nigga and then kissed me?" Raelene wailed.

"'Fraid so." He couldn't help but crack a smile. "Let's go."

As he got ready to hand her off to another agent waiting in the car, Raelene stopped and turned around. "You think you're a big man, but you're not half the man my daddy was," she spat out.

"Yeah. Thank the Lord!" Jesse replied.

EPILOGUE

////////////////////////////////////////////////////////////////////////////////////

*There was* no question that Rosalynn had cold-bloodedly killed Rusty Miller to prevent his testifying at Earl Cooper's trial. Ballistics from the shotgun she had used to end her life matched the shell that killed him. She had called in sick to work that day. A clerk who worked in the DA's office admitted that Rosalynn had sweet-talked him into revealing Rusty's whereabouts while he was trying to impress her with his inside knowledge. He had thought nothing of it, even after Rusty was killed. Wearing a borrowed uniform, Rosalynn had essentially been invisible on the motel grounds. No white man pays any attention to a middle-aged black housekeeper.

Rusty had been killed with a clean shot through a narrow opening. Eddie preferred to think that Rosalynn could have easily killed him that night at Sonny's garage but had chosen to merely scare him away. He would never know the truth.

Sonny and Pearline were relieved to hear about the arrest of Raelene Taylor, the person responsible for terrorizing them. They realized it didn't mean the end of the White Citizens Council and all it stood for, but it was a victory. And that victory was part of the long arc of the moral universe bending toward justice that the Reverend Martin Luther King, Jr. had talked about.

Eddie thought about the words of another "prophet," Sam Cooke, who had sung, "A change is gonna come." When word about the attack had gotten out, it wasn't just black church members who had shown up to provide protection. Some white residents of Ruleville had shown up to offer their help too.

Rosalynn's life may have been stormy, but on the day of her funeral, the sky was robin's-egg blue with brilliant sunshine. Her funeral was held in the same small Baptist church where they had stolen glances at each other as teenagers. Eddie could almost see her smiling teenaged face out of the corner of his eye. Sonny and Pearline sat beside him. He heard Pearline's clear voice when they rose to sing *Amazing Grace*, Rosalynn's favorite hymn.

Eddie had sung it endless times when he was a regular churchgoer. Now the words touched him in a new way, especially the words about being lost and then finally being found.

He had been lost his whole life. He still wasn't sure if he had found Jesus, but he had found a new appreciation for life and felt truly blessed. The blues would no longer be a wall to protect him from his demons but rather a bridge to get to the other side of the crossroads a free man.

Pearline quietly held his hand when the tears ran down his face. Eddie prayed for forgiveness—for himself, for Rosalynn, even for Earl Cooper.

EJ sat apart in the front pew, his fiancée Sandra's arm wrapped around him. Not many of Rosalynn's relatives had shown up, but he was not entirely without family. Matt Cooper sat at the end of the pew, giving EJ his space but showing support. He had quickly accepted EJ as a spiritual if not blood cousin. EJ wanted no part of him. Matt was prepared to wait. Change came slowly in the South.

The red-hot blast from Rosalynn's shotgun had fused Matt and Eddie together as surely as a volcanic eruption created smooth basalt. Had they seen a mother's loving sacrifice for her son or her ultimate expression of contempt? Neither of them could answer that. All Eddie knew was he was glad that the DA had decided to trust the sheriff and made sure he was there when Eddie needed him most.

The FBI had tipped off the sheriff that he had a White Citizens Council mole in his office, although they hadn't been able to determine exactly who it was. Matt had started an investigation to root him or her out. He was determined to transform the sheriff's department and obliterate the last traces of his uncle's hateful legacy.

When Sandra rose after the service, Eddie was surprised to see she was pregnant. Rosalynn must have known. Withholding that joyous piece of news was another way of punishing him.

Eddie tried to approach EJ after the graveside service to talk, but EJ moved away as quickly as if it had been the Devil instead of his father approaching him. Eddie wanted to tell his son that he recognized that shocked, grief-stricken face. It had been his face after Bertie's death. Eddie knew it had taken more than time to heal him. It had taken music, music that poured from his soul. If he couldn't communicate with EJ today, he would work on sharing the music with him any way he could. Eddie was sure EJ would find his way to the blues and eventually to Eddie. At least new fatherhood would fill his life with love.

In the end, the challenging witness prep sessions Eddie endured from the DA were all for nothing. Earl Cooper pleaded guilty to premeditated murder charges the day before the trial was set to start. Maybe he had found true religion as Rosalynn claimed and was ready to accept responsibility for his actions. Or maybe the death of Rosalynn and the revelation that EJ was not his son had broken the spirit of a lonely old man.

DA Dickinson came by in person to tell Eddie about the plea. He brought a surprise.

"What's this?" Eddie asked when Dickinson handed him a check.

"There was a small reward posted by the family for the arrest and conviction of Bertie's killers. I didn't tell you about it because I wanted to make sure you were telling the truth and not offering to testify for money."

"Well, I don't want it."

"Take it, Eddie. The family wants you to have it. And you definitely earned it. Remember, next time you're in town, we've got a date to go fishing."

"Sounds good."

"Oh, yeah, I almost forgot. Webster said to tell you that you were 'right about Clarence Gatemouth Brown,' whatever that means."

"That means Webster's on his way to some new musical horizons," Eddie said with a smile.

The reward wasn't much, but it was enough to cover Eddie's travel expenses home and lost gig money with just enough left over to pay back the loan from Rod Piazza.

Bertie's family had flown down for the trial. After Earl Cooper pled guilty, they testified at the sentencing hearing. They at least had the satisfaction of knowing Bertie's killer would spend the rest of his life in prison with no chance of parole. The family asked to meet with Eddie privately. He haltingly told them what he had witnessed in the barn. Bertie's sister, brother, their spouses, and assorted nieces and nephews eagerly soaked up every word. Finally knowing the details of Bertie's death, gruesome as they were, seemed to provide some kind of closure. Rather than rebuke him for not coming forward sooner, his sister Shemikah thanked him.

"As awful as it was to hear this, it had been almost as painful not knowing what happened. Bless you for finding the courage to talk to us. We'll pray for you. Sending one of his killers to jail will not bring my brother back, but justice will come in another way.

We're going to take the money Mr. Cooper is paying in restitution as part of his plea deal to endow a college scholarship fund in Bertie's name."

Before Eddie left Ruleville, he performed a gospel concert for the Mt. Zion Baptist congregation to show his appreciation for their support. Eddie was surprised at how much he enjoyed performing straight gospel after not playing it for a while. He'd recently heard the "sacred steel" music of the Campbell Brothers. Now he was inspired to dig into it a little deeper. No matter what Sister Gloria and other members thought, blues music was the child of gospel. There wasn't anybody who could pry that mother and child apart.

The good-byes with Sonny and Pearline went easier after he had promised to visit them regularly. They agreed to report back with any news about his grandchild. Eddie wanted to start a Blues in the Schools program through the Blues Foundation in Sunflower County. He'd like to pass on some of Otha's wisdom to future generations of blues musicians. And maybe EJ would approach him on one of his visits.

Sylvia was waiting for him when he got off the bus in LA. They had talked briefly before he left Mississippi, but now they'd be able to have a long conversation about their future face to face. Sylvia had taken the news of EJ and a future grandchild in stride. She still hadn't said "Yes" to his important question, but she hadn't said "Hell no!" either. Eddie was confident they'd be standing before a preacher sometime sooner than later. Reno might be a great place for their wedding. He'd figure out a way to play a little blackjack or do a gig there to pay for it. He'd even bring along Nick as "best man," if he promised not to cry.

Eddie had never played in Europe but had heard there were great audiences there. Maybe he could hook up with an overseas tour and finagle a way to bring Sylvia over to get in a European honeymoon.

Eddie was restless his first night back. He got out of bed at 3:00 am, being careful not to wake Sylvia, and tip-toed into the other room with his guitar. He never thought of himself as much of a songwriter. Tonight though, the words and music for *Bertie's Blues* flowed through him. This much he knew. Blues were the truth and the truth had set him free.

# About the Authors

**Debra Schiff** is a devoted blues fan who can be spotted bopping along to music at blues shows and festivals across the country. She is enjoying retirement after a long career of various types of editorial work. *Murder at the Crossroads* is her second novel. Her first book, *Murder to Scale*, takes place in the world of model railroading.

**Doug Macleod** is a touring recording artist with 36 recordings to his credit. He has been a perennial Blues Music Award nominee and a six-time Blues Music Award winner. Doug is also a songwriter whose songs have been covered by many artists including Eva Cassidy, Albert Collins, and Billy Lee Riley. He was a long-time contributor to *Blues Revue* magazine with his column *Doug's Back Porch*.